Writing the Cozy Myst

Writing the Cozy Mystery

Authors' Perspectives on Their Craft

Edited by
PHYLLIS M. BETZ

McFarland & Company, Inc., Publishers
Jefferson, North Carolina

LIBRARY OF CONGRESS CATALOGUING-IN-PUBLICATION DATA

Names: Betz, Phyllis M. (Phyllis Marie), 1953– editor.
Title: Writing the cozy mystery : authors' perspectives on their craft /
    edited by Phyllis M. Betz.
Description: Jefferson, North Carolina : McFarland & Company, Inc., Publishers, 2024. |
    Includes bibliographical references and index.
Identifiers: LCCN 2024030452 | ISBN 9781476690827 (paperback : acid free paper) ∞
    ISBN 9781476654263 (ebook)
Subjects: LCSH: Detective and mystery stories—Authorship. | Cozy mystery stories—
    Authorship. | LCGFT: Essays.
Classification: LCC PN3377.5.D4 W73 2024 | DDC 808.3/872—dc23/eng/20240708
LC record available at https://lccn.loc.gov/2024030452

BRITISH LIBRARY CATALOGUING DATA ARE AVAILABLE

ISBN (print) 978-1-4766-9082-7
ISBN (ebook) 978-1-4766-5426-3

Front cover image © Creative Lab/Shutterstock

Printed in the United States of America

McFarland & Company, Inc., Publishers
   Box 611, Jefferson, North Carolina 28640
   www.mcfarlandpub.com

For Marty Knepper and Molly Freier
My partners in crime

Acknowledgments

My first thanks go to Sherry Harris; she has been a strong and enthusiastic supporter of this present volume as well as *Reading the Cozy Mystery.* She allowed me space on the wickedauthors.com blog to place an announcement to solicit contributions for this collection.

All of the authors who took time from their busy schedules to offer their descriptions of how they approach writing their novels must be thanked. I also want to thank them for their patience as the collection has worked its way through the process of turning ideas into a finished book.

And, it goes without saying, thanks to Joan, my constant cheerleader and support.

Table of Contents

Introduction

Give the Cozy Its Due

Phyllis M. Betz

Why, when the cozy mystery has become one of the most popular and best-selling categories in the publishing world, do so many commentators and critics still pay it short shrift? Even the most cursory Google search will pull up millions of sites dedicated to the cozy mystery. Recently I typed in the phrase cozy mystery and in .61 seconds had 9,370,000 hits (May 12, 2023). Granted, there will be duplications in the sites available for viewing, but such an extraordinary number in so short a time does speak to the constantly growing popularity of this mystery subgenre. The emphasis of such sites include bookstores, author pages, fan blogs, reviews, and lists. One of the most popular cozy mystery sites, cozy-mystery.com, offers one of the more comprehensive places to discover the world of cozy novels and novelists. The viewer can find alphabetical lists of authors, as well as a breakdown of the most common thematic emphases in the subgenre—animals, crafts, historical, the supernatural and much more. The site also lists television shows and movies based on cozy mysteries. In addition to sites like this, other more traditional crime fiction sites give room to the cozy; crimereads.com, for example, has 35 pages of articles devoted to the cozy. These articles include reviews and commentary from well-known mystery authors and critics, as well as lists of newly published works. In spite of such evidence of the appeal of the cozy mystery, the overall response to these texts still remains muted at best.

In 1992, Marilyn Stasio, mystery critic for *The New York Times Book Review*, wrote a critique of the subgenre that has become a standard starting point for discussions of cozy: "Murder Least Foul: The Cozy, Soft-Boiled Mystery." Stasio offers a definition of the cozy that still operates for modern writers and readers: the absence of violence, an amateur detective and the emphasis on community and personal relationships (Stasio). She places cozy within the larger context of the classic British detective novel, but then turns to a critique that emphasizes the cozy's overall weaknesses compared to its predecessors:

> The de-emphasis of the puzzle plot is surely the most important of these changes. For Sayers, Christie and other author-architects of the classic form, the essence of the detective story was its well-designed plot, one that posed an intellectual puzzle whose solution turned on the logical principles of deductive reasoning. In the contemporary cozy, however, deduction takes second place.... By oversimplifying the plot through the elimination of its trickier puzzle elements, cozy authors have also reduced the complexity of the crime-solving process and diminished the detective's intellectual role in that cognitive process [Stasio].

The cozy, Stasio suggests, watered down those attributes that attract the reader to a mystery story. Besides presenting simplified plots, Stasio notes the cozy's foregrounding of the characters, particularly the female protagonist, over the sleuthing of the detective, usually a man, who tends to be a member of the police force or a professional investigator. These shifts in the cozy mystery narrative, Stasio cautions, may have a detrimental impact on the detective novel by undermining those qualities that determine its lasting impact on readers.

Granted that Marilyn Stasio's article appeared at the beginning of the cozy's entry into the public's interest in the form, the influence of her discussion has had a long-lasting impact on subsequent commentary on the cozy. In the 2021 September issue *The Atlantic Monthly* Alyse Burnside engages with how the cozy mystery minimizes the introduction of violence into its pages; she begins from the truism that violence in cozy mysteries tends to be relegated to the margins of the story, which allows readers to "immerse themselves in a world of crime without worrying that they will be overcome with unpleasant images of real grief; they choose to glimpse violence precisely so they can look away [which] alleviates the need to interrogate what is so seductive to humans about violence" (Burnside). By *disappearing* violence, Burnside states that the cozy thus builds a barrier between the reader and the real world. Burnside readily admits that her own fascination with true crime also encourages a belief that she will be able to contain the fears that violence evokes, but the "impossibly quaint" characteristics of the cozy keep the real world of violence at bay.

Stasio's statement that the cozy presents an uncomplicated plotline is belied by the many cozy mysteries that combine multiple subplots; for example, in Leslie Budewitz's *Assault and Pepper*, the search for the murderer of a homeless man in the doorway to Pepper Reece's spice shop begins when the police accuse Sam, another homeless man, of the murder. Pepper's investigation to prove Sam's innocence becomes complicated by a web of other characters' connections to Pepper and the victim and suspect. The relationship of Tory Finch, one of Pepper's employees, to the deceased redirects Pepper's investigation when it is discovered she is the daughter of the murdered man. The victim's business partner, as well as his ex-wife, also become suspects. After a series of misdirections and missteps, Pepper discovers the true culprit, someone who originally seemed totally unconnected to the crime, but who had had a previous connection to the victim. However, these several threads are woven into a clear resolution at the novel's conclusion. This multi-layered structure typifies many cozy narratives and serves not only to develop the plot, but also to describe the community in which the crime occurs. It is this emphasis on the protagonist's relationships, I believe, that many commentators on the cozy find problematic.

The cozy narrative does highlight the protagonist's many relationships presented over the course of a novel. Whether these are personal—close friends or family—or social—clients or customers (since many main characters own businesses)—such connections provide depth to the depiction of the characters. Over a series, these individuals and their lives will become more fully developed as the main character's social circle expands. The protagonist frequently relies on these relationships to further her search for the killer, since she does not have access to the range of investigative tools available to the police. Pepper Reece, as a new owner in Seattle's Pike Place Market, learns not only the ins and outs of the Market's community of shop owners, but also utilizes others' knowledge and skills in pursuit of the investigation. Pepper also relies on her good friend Kristen Gardiner's sympathy and advice throughout the course of the novel. I would suggest that the cozy is no different from other mystery subgenres: Christie's Miss Marple's and Hercule Poirot's investigations are filled with red herrings and supposed killers who are revealed to be innocent; the denouement at the conclusion of a typical Christie novel presents the unraveling of sometimes exquisitely complex plots. Interestingly, Christie's Marple and Poirot novels lack a fully realized sense of the characters' home environments: St. Mary Mead is the location for only three of Miss Marple's investigations, but the descriptions of the village and her social circle are minimal. While Poirot's base is London, his investigations often take him far beyond his home. Poirot does have Captain Hastings with whom he can discuss a case, but more typically Hasting's advice or comments are given short shrift by Poirot. Surprisingly, Miss Marple has no friend to confide in or discuss her investigation; like the goddess Nemesis, Miss Marple is the solitary pursuer of justice.

Stasio's comment that the cozy discards the classical investigative practices of its predecessors rings false as well; the cozy protagonist observes the murder scene, looks for clues, and interrogates suspects and witnesses to tease out fact from fiction just as most traditional detectives do. Isn't this a description of Poirot's approach to solving the murder?

Don't many of Miss Marple's conclusions arise from her intuitive understanding of human nature? George Dove's criteria for what constitutes a detective story easily apply to the cozy as well as to other mystery narratives: the main character is a detective, regardless of gender and whether they are a professional or an amateur; the narrative is built around the investigation of the crime, although other subplots may be included; the mystery is complex and seems incapable of being solved; the reader may be able to solve the crime before the novel's investigator if the author adheres to the conventions of the genre (10). Pepper Reece may be a reluctant detective at first, but once she commits herself to solving Doc's murder, she takes on the attitudes and behaviors of every detective who has preceded her. It is not a surprise, then, that in the subsequent novels in the Spice Shop Mystery Series Pepper becomes more adept as an investigator.

Burnside's contention that cozy mysteries dilute the impact of violence is also short-sighted. As in all detective fiction, whatever the subgenre, a death is the instigator to everything that follows. What distinguishes the cozy from these other types of crime novels is the representation of that death and violence. Typically, the actual murder of the victim has occurred off-stage, although not always at the beginning of a novel, and the scene of the murder lacks the bloody detail of other mystery subgenres. I think it is fair to note that in many classic murder mysteries, the death also often occurs off-stage—or out of the view of other characters—and is presented in a more bloodless manner. The proliferation of violence and the sometimes–hyper-realistic description of violence has become a hallmark of certain subgenres of mystery fiction in the last decades of the twentieth century. The murder is often committed in front of the reader and the details of the scene are grotesquely described. However, the means of death in many cozies *is* often disturbing; in addition to blunt objects, poison, and other traditional methods, cozy victims, for example, have been impaled with knitting needles. Cozies are also not immune to violence; a reader will find characters who are threatened with harm or attacked by a suspect. Pepper Reece, for instance, is attacked once by the actual murderer in *Assault and Pepper*. Where readers of hard-boiled, noir, or serial murder will see the mangled, bloody body of the victim as well as the bruised face of the detective, such descriptions are typically left out of the cozy. This does not mean that the consequences of violence are overlooked. At the end of *Assault and Pepper*, after the perpetrator in identified and arrested, Pepper is still limping from the attack.

A lack of explicit detail, however, does not negate the impact of the victim's demise. When Pepper Reece discovers the body of Doc Finch in the doorway of her shop, she experiences a range of emotions—shock, anger, and fear. But the cozy detective manages to refocus her initial paralysis into action; Pepper, for instance, becomes determined and driven to save Sam by solving Doc's death. This is not to suggest that Pepper or any other cozy protagonist is suddenly fearless and goes headlong into the chase. Here is the value of the community in which the protagonist lives; good friends often become the voice of reason and caution. Burnside's second point of contention, that the world of the cozy sugarcoats the harsher realities of the world the characters inhabit, underscores the common view of the cozy as a throwaway subgenre. While some cozies do situate their narratives in very closed, almost-perfect settings, modern cozy writers do not turn away from serious social issues. Budewitz has included descriptions of the tension between the upscale consumers of the Pike Place Market and trendy Seattle neighborhoods and the original residents of the Market area; her novel also describes characters who do not enjoy the privileges of social status. Sam, the individual initially accused of murdering Doc, is one of the homeless people who come to the Market to ask for handouts. Sam is also a veteran who suffers from some mental disorder, perhaps PTSD, which complicates his interactions with the police. Budewitz is also careful to describe the diverse races and ethnicities who live in the area. Again, although keeping the time and place that Christie's novels take place in mind, their settings portray the more sanitized environment typically applied to the cozy. Often in these works, the introduction of an outsider character, whether of a different race or ethnicity, marks that individual as suspect, if not actual murderer. This awareness of the multiplicities of a cozy's setting and characters has become a common feature of contemporary cozies.

Burnside's comment that readers of cozies participate in violence without acknowledging its consequences makes the cozy reader out to be rather heartless. The attraction of a reader to death and violence must not be taken as a sign of a reader's pathology; Burnside admits that she herself is fascinated with true crime stories, a narrative form that frequently emphasizes violent murders, serial killers, and corruption. Yet, she does not in her essay deny the power of violence to impact a reader. She has indicated that her attraction to violence offers a way for her to "parse my greatest fears through grim exposure therapy. By wallowing in the very worst of the world, I convince myself that I'm taking control of the vilest possibilities, rationing out my fear until it feels tamable" (Burnside). Is this any different from the cozy reader who sees the terrible cruelty that exists in the world and finds in a protagonist a way to take control of the fear that no one is invulnerable to the possibility of violence? The cozy protagonist is often seen as a type of common-woman figure, an ordinary person thrown into searching for a killer by accident. Cozy mystery readers see the protagonist as relatable because she has no extraordinary abilities that make her stand out from her community. She will draw on her circle of friends, use her knowledge or skills based on her interests or profession, and with the assistance of the police bring about the satisfying conclusion that all detective stories provide.

Wayne Johnson, in the essay "The Two Camps of Crime: Christie's Cool, Cozy Tales of Ratiocination and Highsmith's Psycho-Sexual Deep Waters," describes the term "cozy" as a way for the reader to discover "*psychic distance*, a safe, comfortable place from which the reader experiences the actions of the story" (italics in text). He suggests that this comfort is rooted in the investigative practices of the traditional mystery. At the core of these narratives is the thinking detective, who uses keen observation and logical analysis to determine the solution to the crime; through his or her efforts, the correct outcome is achieved and, thus, restores a sense of order to the community that the original crime disrupted. This requirement in the detective demands an emotional distance from both the crime and the other characters involved in their investigation; without this detachment the detective cannot concentrate on the puzzle that the crime represents. Johnson constantly emphasizes the novel's form, the "*construct*," of the plot which supersedes the more emotional aspects of a character (italics in text). Johnson summarizes this view by noting "[t]hese stories are *about* the larger human story—not *of* it. All is witnessed at a safe remove ... because in this lineage of crime fiction, even the irrational is subsumed by the larger and entirely comprehensible meaning: ... the irrational is contained within the soon to be entirely comprehensible (rational) story" (Johnson, italics in text). Johnson's insistence on the emotional distance of the detective from the investigation of deliberate murder reinforces Burnside's assertion regarding the cozy mystery's diluted representation of violence. While they do show that murder is a disruption of social order, neither Miss Marple nor Hercule Poirot seem to exhibit an intense emotional response to the deaths they encounter. Murderers receive little sympathy for their actions, and even other individuals caught up in the investigation are viewed more for how they add to or hinder the pursuit of justice. Interestingly, both Poirot and Miss Marple do show a softness toward young men and women who have a romantic attachment.

The cozy protagonist does respond emotionally to the crime, particularly to victims who have no reason to be killed or particularly to characters who behave suspiciously or antagonistically to authorities. Sam has been presumed guilty from the moment Doc's body is found as there had been some disagreement between him and Doc. Sam's reluctance and fear of the police adds to their insistence that he is guilty; in addition, Sam's mental disorder exacerbates his interaction with them, which reinforces their belief in Sam's guilt. Tory, Doc's daughter, also comes under suspicion for her father's death, but Pepper's investigations prove that she is another intended target of the real murderer. Sam's race (he is African American) may also contribute to the police's focus on him as the suspect. The protagonist's emotional life is often viewed as a drawback by some critics. Her friendships and romantic attachments disrupt the progress of the investigation and add confusion as to the actual purpose of the narrative. Many commentators assert that these types of connections can push the criminal investigation to the background of the story. The cozy's inclusion of a developing romance between the protagonist and the police officer connected to the case is a standard convention, but Lord Peter Wimsey's attraction to, growing involvement with, and eventual marriage to Harriet Vane generally is not seen as a disadvantage in his investigations.

The categorization of the cozy mystery as a woman's novel has always opened the subgenre to complaints from critics that these are not works to be taken seriously. Yet, the most famous Golden Age mystery writers were women—Agatha Christie, Dorothy Sayers, Margery Allingham, Josephine Tey, and Ngaio Marsh. When women writers took on forms that were considered the purview of male writers, like the hard-boiled detective, they faced many harsh, negative responses, even when writers like Sara Paretsky, Marcia Muller, Lauren Douglas Wright, among many, mastered the form. Today, more and more male writers, such as Richard Osman and Alexander McCall Smith, are venturing into the cozy subgenre. Cozy writers, it is also said, cannot be taken seriously because they rely heavily on the conventions of the detective story to develop characters and plot, but as George Dove, John Cawelti, and other analysts of the genre note, all detective fiction, whatever the narrative focus, rely on sets of expected tropes that mark the form and distinguish one from another. Whatever the narrative frame, however, the traditional detective, the noir protagonist, the police officer, all engage in the shared essential structure of a death, a detective, an investigation, and a resolution. Cozy mysteries are no different from their predecessors and contemporaries, and this collection sets out to show that the cozy mystery more than deserves to be part of that community by letting cozy authors describe what they do to create their work.

One of my constant questions about a text often centers on how writers make the necessary choices that will help them accomplish their goal—producing a novel that attracts a variety of readers. Basically, I make educated guesses built on my experience as a critic and a reader; sometimes I am lucky enough to find source materials that support my ideas about the text. This, after all, is what critics do: find as much primary and secondary material about a work or an author and try to develop a cogent idea about motives and methods. Even in this situation, though, I am still interpretating what I have read, and I am aware of the danger of falling into the trap of intentional fallacy, making assumptions about an author's intentions based on personal bias or interest. Sometimes all a critic has is the work itself and, if I'm lucky, a few reviews or comments. Sometimes a critic is fortunate to discover information, ideally from the writers themselves, that provides a clear description of their intentions and how they go about embodying them. One of the best sources for any critic is to have writers' own descriptions of how their creative process works; writers, after all, know best how to devise an exciting plot, create compelling characters, and devise a satisfying resolution. They also are aware of keeping their work fresh while maintaining their audience. Cozy writers are especially attuned to the requirements of their genre as well as the desires of their readers, and in the essays that follow, they present their methods and illustrate that they, like all mystery writers, are not only masters of their craft but also artists who challenge themselves to create mysteries that expand their audience.

The collection is divided into four general categories. "Writing Genre" presents authors' examinations of what makes a cozy a cozy as well as discussions of their choice to write a cozy mystery. "Writing Theme" focuses on the particular skill a protagonist uses or profession he or she has as well explores social issues, including diversity. "Writing Setting" considers the settings and how they play in the work. "Writing Character" addresses developing a range of characters, especially protagonists, who embody non-traditional qualities or who are typically not seen as belonging in the cozy. However, these categories are permeable as a discussion of social issues, for instance, will examine the setting in which a conflict is placed. Talking about character development brings in dealing with expanding concepts of the cozy's literary antecedents.

Cozy writers are very aware of the negative criticism that is attached to their chosen approach to writing mysteries. Sherry Harris' essay, "In Defense of Cozy Mysteries," acts as the foundation for the essays that follow. In it she asserts the cozy's right to be taken seriously because this subgenre, just like any other mystery narrative, is developed by the writer's adherence to the specific criteria necessary to fulfill its subgenre. Building her rebuttal to the critics, Harris demonstrates that the conventions needed to write a successful cozy mystery demand the same attention to detail and innovation expected of any mystery novelist. After Harris, two essays deal specifically with the authors' choice of the cozy as their preferred narrative structure. Both Vicki Delany ("Why I Became a Cozy Writer—And Why I'm Happy I Did") and Justin M. Kiska ("From Following the Rules and Regs to Throwing Them Out the Window") find in the cozy mystery an opportunity to reframe their experience with other subgenres. Delany and Kisko point out the freedom that the cozy allows them to escape from the rigidity of their other mystery series: for Delany, it was the heavy toll that the violence in her psychological suspense and her police procedurals had on her; for Kisko, it's not having to follow the investigative and procedural demands of his police novels. Both writers also note that the cozy gave them the chance to bring a light-heartedness to their mysteries that was missing from their earlier works. In "Crimes of Fashion" Diane Vallere takes a more humorous view of her decision to take up writing her cozy mysteries. If a writer should use what she knows as the foundation for her work, Vallere's previous position in the luxury fashion industry provides her with a rich source of material and also gives her the opportunity to present the comic side of the field and the behavior of those who work in it.

While the definition of the cozy mystery makes its appearance in most of the collections's essays, Kait Carson's ("Where Subgenres Overlap") and Tina deBellegarde's ("Cozy and Not-So-Cozy Novels: Defying a Sub-Genre Label") tackle the exact nature of the form head on. Carson takes issue with the difficulties of defining the cozy by highlighting the problem of how to categorize it, since many cozy mysteries share methods and practices of other detective novels. Carson illustrates these challenges by describing how she wrestles with the dilemma of where her mysteries fit. Carson looks at the relationship between the traditional mystery and the cozy, and her essay describes how she engages with both to develop the approach she finds most successful. Mary Anna Evans in "Stepping Out of the Shadow of the Queen of Crime" engages with the definition of the cozy by examining the power of Agatha Christie's influence on the mystery genre. Evans examines the far-reaching impact Christie has had not only on the mystery but on culture as well. Evans also points out that, as a writer of mysteries herself, she must come to terms with Christie's stature in the world of the mystery.

Cozy authors know that the cozy needs to adhere to the standards that every mystery novel must as well as utilize those specific to the subgenre to create a work that attracts readers. J.A. Hennrikus, in "Fair Play in Cozies," focuses on one of the essential conventions of the detective novel: the idea of fair play—the requirement that the author presents readers with all of the necessary information about the crime and suspects, so that the detective's revelation of the perpetrator is credible. Hennrikus first provides some background on the traditional detective novel's use of conventions and then compares how the cozy author adapts them to fit the specific needs of the form. Andrea J. Johnson in "The Accessibility of Cozies: How Playing Fair Is How Cozies Endure" also examines how important the concept of fair play is to the development of the cozy mystery. In addition to understanding how a mystery works and why, Johnson illustrates how maintaining the standards of fair play encourages the reader to feel fully engaged with the protagonist's search for the truth. Knowing the writer is providing the necessary technical components required for the mystery to work gives the reader the opportunity to become caught up in the characters and their involvement with the crime and pursuit.

Peggy Ehrhart's "From Rue Morgue to the Craft Cozy: The Evolution of the Traditional Mystery" also examines how cozy writers take the traditional mystery's conventions and build on them for their own work. She does this by discussing the way cozies have utilized crafts in the narratives. Craft, as Erhart notes, includes a character's identity, business, or hobby, and the aspect emphasized in the work impacts how the protagonist can use the accompanying skills and knowledge to solve the crime. The key is to make certain that the descriptions of the character's craft does not overwhelm the development of the plot.

Many cozy writers are able to juggle multiple series, sometimes simultaneously, which some critics tend to see as detrimental; they often point to the over-reliance on the conventional requirements of plot and character at the expense of creating compelling stories. Edith Maxwell ("Writing Multiple Series") breaks down the process: describing the technical aspects of time management and maintaining a schedule of writing and editing as well as dealing with publishing issues. Most important is for the writer to keep their series separate from one another by emphasizing the specific settings and characters for each series.

A hallmark of the cozy is an author giving the protagonist some particular skill or talent that often allows them to establish a business which will prove useful in their investigation. Sybil Johnson, in "Crafts and the Cozy Mystery," makes her protagonist a freelance computer programmer. This gives Johnson's detective the ability to balance work demands with the pursuit of an investigation. In addition to her computer skills, the protagonist also enjoys painting, which becomes the source for many of the investigations she is involved in. Food preparation is, perhaps, one of the most common skills presented in cozy mysteries. Maya Corrigan, in her essay "'Cookies open doors': Food as an Investigative Tool," discusses how she has developed her series around a protagonist who owns a small café and, with the help of her grandfather, pursues crimes that revolve around the prepping, serving, and eating of food.

Modern cozy writers have become more conscious of how social changes can impact the development of characters, descriptions of settings, and the complications of the protagonist's investigations. Leslie Budewitz's essay, "Writing the World Around Us: Social Issues in the Cozy," explores the social consequences that crime has on a community and the role the protagonist plays in bringing order back to that community. She notes how many contemporary cozy writers link the criminal's actions to these social ills. Budewitz also emphasizes the protagonist's awareness of or involvement with the darker aspects of society and how they often shape their response to the crime and their commitment to pursuing an investigation. In "Cultural Elements Elevate a Cozy Mystery," Jennifer J. Chow highlights the importance of creating characters who reflect the diversity of the real world. Such expansion gives a reader greater insight into the protagonist's personality in addition to utilizing cultural differences to add to the tension in the protagonist's investigation.

The mystery's setting is an essential feature of any novel; the setting helps establish the mood of the novel overall and provides insight into characters' personalities and behaviors. Rabbi Ilene Schneider in "Mise en Scène" focuses on how cozy writers decide not only on where to set the novel but also how to describe it in order to catch readers' attention and maintain their interest. The most important aspects of choosing a setting reflect the writer's background—the places they have lived, for example—the amount of research needed to establish its believability, and the place's suitability to the needs of the story. A writer must also consider how much descriptive detail to include: too much detracts from the focus on the mystery, too little renders the scene generic. Finding the right balance contributes to a work that pulls the reader into the narrative.

How many murders can take place in a small town? The cozy's small-town setting is often seen as a detriment to the development of the storyline, especially in cozy mystery series. What has been called the Cabot Cove Syndrome, where the murder (or murders) that take place in the town would realistically reduce its population, contributes to the perceived lack of realism and credulity in the novels. As Marni Graff points out in "Handling Diverse Settings" writers pay close attention to the creation of a book's setting, often visiting locations, conducting research, or using local residents to construct the places where the novel is set. While the descriptions of setting may make changes to the actual place, these alterations do not affect the credibility of such portrayals. In fact, as Graff points out, the importance of getting the scene right adds to the characters' engagement in the events of the story. Just as a protagonist's skill with a craft can aid in the solution to the crime, their knowledge of the scene helps in discovering the connection between a suspect or criminal to the investigation.

M.E. Hilliard offers a new approach to the role setting plays in the cozy mystery. In "Cozy Crime in a Surveillance Society" Hilliard examines the challenges that the technology of surveillance offers the writer. She notes the growing presence of cameras used by the police and individuals even in small towns. Today, practically everyone uses cell phones and social media which can impact the development of the story and, particularly, the investigation. As Hilliard states, even an amateur detective can access a great deal of information with a basic technical ability. Hilliard is quick to stress that even with the proliferation of cameras the writer can still devise an effective mystery.

Every mystery novel demands that the protagonist embody the traits generally seen as necessary for the successful identification and capture of the criminal. Cozies receive much criticism for the prominence of the protagonist at the expense of the progress of the investigation; in addition, the cozy detective, most likely because they are amateurs, are seen as two-dimensional figures who lack any investigative skill. Amanda Flower addresses such complaints in her essay "What Makes a Cozy Character." Flower lays out the criteria she offers as the building blocks for creating compelling protagonists. The essay highlights the internal qualities of the character's personality that give her the desire and ability to become involved in solving the crime; these include curiosity about the events at the center of the mystery; the ability to balance work demands and investigating; a strong sense of justice and a willingness to pursue the search for the criminal; and the ability to evaluate clues and suspects to arrive at the solution. In addition to the personal aspects of the protagonists' character, Flower makes reference to the social environment in which the protagonist moves, which includes friends, romantic partners, and even pets. Flower takes care to note that cozy characters should not be static figures but open to adaptation.

The next essays illustrate Flower's assertion that characters must reflect the time and place in which they function. "...And a Colorful Cast: Building a Diverse Cozy" by Kathleen Marple Kalb (Nikki Knight) stresses the increasing presence of diverse characters in cozy mysteries, reflecting the diversity of their authors. The cozy protagonist will be Asian or Latin or African American; will be gay or lesbian or older; will be physically challenged or neurologically divergent; or will confront addictions or face other challenges. Kalb also points out the need for the author to take care in the development of such characters, that the writer must not include a person of color, for example, just to check off a box. The author's responsibility remains centered on making sure that a particular character fits the circumstances of the novel.

J.C. Kenney reminds readers in "I'm Okay, Really: Writing a Main Character Who Has an Addiction or a Mental Health Disorder" that cozy protagonists are not extraordinary heroes; rather, they are normal individuals who are thrown into extraordinary situations, and the majority of cozy protagonists work their way through the mystery with little to impede their efforts. However, some cozy protagonists must deal with the debilitating effects of personal struggles with addiction or mental health challenges like anxiety or depression. A character experiencing such challenges would seem unlikely to be able to take on an investigation such a murder. However, Kenney points out that these characters' battles have given them the skills and tenacity to follow the search for the criminal to the end. Carol E. Ayer also writes of a protagonist who experiences the world differently in "Writing a Highly Sensitive Amateur Sleuth." Ayer describes how her protagonist must maneuver her way through an investigation when her highly sensitive nature radically impacts her ability to pursue it. Ayer's protagonist does not veer too far away from the typical depiction of the cozy protagonist; she has a career, a small circle of friends, and a romantic interest. Not surprisingly, the sensitivity that could be an impediment to solving the crime provides Ayer's protagonist the skills needed to overcome the challenges to a successful resolution.

Winnie Frolik's "Why I Wrote a Buddy Cop Series with a Lesbian and a Jew" presents another illustration of how contemporary cozy writers have expanded the range of character representation in their work. Pointing out that mystery novels deal with secrets, Frolik creates protagonists whose own secrets, their sexual identities and religion, add complexity to their characters and to how they conduct their investigations. Frolik also places her characters in a setting, 1930s England, that presents a real threat to their lives, showing how the concerns of the past still resonate in the present.

I have selected these essays because they reveal the amazing talents of their writers. The commitment to producing novels that appeal to a wide audience comes through as each discusses the attraction of the subgenre and how they continually work to develop its potential by devising intricate plots, creating attractive characters, and striving to keep the cozy fresh As Sherry Harris affirms, "Cozy mysteries don't need defense, they need respect."

Works Cited

Budewitz, Leslie. *Assault and Pepper*. The Berkley Publishing Group, 2015.
Burnside, Alyse. "The Dark Reality Behind 'Cozy Mysteries.'" *The Atlantic*, September 16, 2021. September 23, 2023. https://www.theatlantic.com.
Dove, George. *The Reader and the Detective Story*. Bowling Green State University Popular Press, 1997.
Johnson, Wayne. "The Two Camps of Crime: Christie's Cool, Cozy Tales of Ratiocination and Highsmith's Psycho-Sexual Deep Waters." CrimeReads, March 16, 2022. April 23, 2023. https://crimereads.com/christie-highsmith-crime-fiction-deep-waters.
Stasio, Marilyn. "Murder Least Foul: The Cozy, Soft-Boiled Mystery." *New York Times*, October 18, 1992. https://www.nytimes,com/1992/10/18/books/crime-mystery-murder-least-foul-the-cozy-soft-boiled-mystery.html.

PART ONE

Writing Genre

In Defense of Cozy Mysteries

Sherry Harris

In the spring of 2019, I came home after attending several crime-writing conferences. For some reason there were more people attacking cozy mysteries than usual. Frankly, I was discouraged and angry. The crime fiction community is generally a supportive one; however, that spring I'd been on a number of panels where other authors were dismissive of the value of the cozy mystery and seemed to think cozies were easy to write.

The criticism came in many forms: someone on a panel sneering as they said, "Oh, I don't write cozies," as if it was beneath them, or an author making fun of the often punny titles on their social media, or someone dismissing the happy-looking covers or delving into what they called the tropes of cozy mysteries. I walked out of one panel to hear a cop, who'd been in the audience, say to his friend, "Whew, we can swear now," followed by raucous laughter.

Cozy mysteries are beloved by many and scorned by some. What is a cozy? It's a book with an amateur sleuth who usually runs a business (like Sarah Winston who runs garage sales in my books), set in a small town or close-knit neighborhood in a city, with a mystery (usually a murder) at its core. The amateur sleuth has a compelling reason to solve the mystery, like the death of a friend or a friend who is accused of murder, and often has help from a set of quirky secondary characters.

Barbara Ross, in her essay titled "How I Learned to Relax About Being a 'Cozy' Author and Just Write the Damn Books—Part III," asks: "The question was, can a cozy be good crime fiction? Was it a reasonable question? I think it was. After all, a cozy has never won an Edgar® Award for Best Novel[1] and most cozy writers believe one never will. So why would I want to work this hard at something a whole lot of people—to be clear, people whom I like and respect as writers—think can never be 'good'?"

Sandra Jackson-Opoku[2] recently said on a panel that cozies are the "disregarded stepchild of crime fiction." But why is that? The common criticisms I've heard include the use of tropes, the "light" storylines, and, as I mentioned above, the cover art and titles with puns.

Book covers are signals that to some degree tell you what's inside a book. Most cozy mysteries have covers that are pretty and/or fun. They are usually designed with cheery colors; there's rarely a weapon or blood. Julia Henry's Garden Squad covers and Maddie Day's Cape Cod covers are prime examples. Both make one think, "I want to be in that place"—not "I want the bejesus scared out of me."

Book covers created a problem for me when I did a book signing at a major bookseller. Due to some unfortunate timing, they put me in their children's section because they were moving things around on the adult side of the store. Because of the cheery covers for my Sarah Winston Garage Sale mysteries, complete with a cat, people thought they were children's books. I spent the entire two hours telling people not to buy my books and no, their child shouldn't read them.

I was recently on a panel at a crime fiction conference and heard this: "In the same way that some people say they 'don't like horror movies' or 'don't like jazz music,' some readers will say that they 'don't like cozies.' I'd be surprised if we had any of those folks here in the room, but it's quite likely that the people who are here know people who claim not to like cozies. What should they tell those heretics to motivate them to give your books a try?"

My answer was simple. "Don't judge a book by its fluffy cover." And while the answer was a bit flippant, I was dead serious. There are a number of cozy writers who tackle important issues in their books. My Sarah Winston Garage Sale mysteries look at how the spouses and children of active-duty military are impacted. *Absence of Alice* looks at the hoops military families with special needs children have to go through to get help. In *Devil's Chew Toy* by Rob Osler the sleuth and his friends fear the police won't work hard on a case involving a missing gay man who's also a Dreamer so they feel compelled to try to find him themselves.

In a recent email to me Barbara Ross said, "I don't so much tackle issues, but they exist in the world and my characters must deal with them. There's income inequality in *Muddled Through*. Drug addiction and prescription drug costs in the US in *Musseled Out*. Legal and illegal immigration in *Sealed Off* and climate change in many of the books as lobstermen and clammers must deal with the warming Gulf of Maine." Cozy mystery authors, like any other crime fiction author, balance issues in contemporary society along with plot.

Cozy mysteries are known for their titles with puns, and they are another indicator of what type of book the reader will experience. Donna

Andrews combines a bird with a pun and comes up with clever titles like *Gone Gulls* and *Die Like an Eagle*. In my Sarah Winston books there are *I Know What You Bid Last Summer* and *Let's Fake a Deal* and in my Chloe Jackson Sea Glass Saloon series *From Beer to Eternity* and *A Time to Swill*. As with the covers, the titles don't mean there is no substance in the book.

But cozies have tropes! Cue the pearl clutching. I'm sorry but all genre fiction has tropes—we'll talk more about that later. What are some of the tropes in cozies? As I said above, almost all cozy protagonists are amateur sleuths who run some kind of business. Meri Allen's protagonist manages an ice cream shop; Mia P. Manansala's protagonist runs a café; and, uniquely, Raquel Reyes's protagonist is a food anthropologist with a TV show.

In many cozy mysteries the amateur sleuth returns to their hometown to help with a family business. Cozies usually have some humor and romance. The protagonist often has a romantic connection to someone in law enforcement. They live in a small town that all of us are going to want to live in—except for the murder rates in these villages. Rest assured, though, the amateur sleuth will solve the murder. Justice will prevail and there will be a happy ending. While tropes are part of all genre fiction, they don't define them, and I find that especially true in cozy mysteries.

There are other misconceptions such as men don't read cozies—any cozy author will tell you this simply isn't true. Yet the myth perpetuates that cozies are written only by women for women. And that somehow makes them less than. Critics also say reading a cozy is the equivalent of eating cotton candy—they are all fluff and no substance. Cozies run the gamut from very fluffy where the author creates an idyllic town where only a "bad" person dies to the more traditional side where no one deserves to die but someone does.

Like most cozy authors I try to write books that fit the parameters of the genre but also have emotional depth with complex male and female characters who are trying to live their lives when a murder interrupts it. And frankly, I think my Sarah Winston, like most cozy writers' protagonists, is as real or more real than many of the characters we see in thrillers. But I don't mock writers who have protagonists who can beat up five men blindfolded, after they've been stabbed, shot at, run over, and tortured. Critics of the cozy act as if these characters are more realistic than a shop owner who tries to help her friend get cleared of a crime.

All genre fiction has tropes. Suspense and domestic suspense often deal with intimate family or neighborhood settings. They usually have an unreliable narrator or information that is withheld in the beginning of the novel to create a big twist near the end. Action thrillers almost always have an alpha male or female protagonist. These people seemingly can go for days without sleep or food and be beaten to a pulp but bounce right back. Noir has the tarnished private eye with personal problems.

All writing is hard work, from poetry to romance to sci fi to crime fiction which makes those who look down their noses at cozy mysteries particularly hard to take. What does make a cozy hard to write? The mystery writer is in a battle of wits with their readers. They have to lay everything out so that the mystery can be solved by the protagonist and the reader, but do it in such a way the reader can't figure it out before the protagonist does.

A cozy protagonist doesn't have mad skills. They haven't been in the CIA, aren't Navy Seals, and don't have any special training. They are more likely to have a bum knee than be a martial arts expert. They are regular people caught up in extraordinary circumstances.

They don't have access to equipment. No helicopters, flame-throwers, or automatic weapons are at their disposal. Our protagonists only have their wits and their cell phones. Okay, maybe they have a laptop and knitting needles too, but that's it. What else makes a cozy harder to write?

Access to information—oh, how nice it would be to have my protagonist call her contact at the CIA who's willing to break the law and share information with her. She would be happy to be able to call someone at the police department, but I've set up an antagonistic relationship with the police so she can't even do that. Cozy protagonists must piece together bits of information to come up with a solution.

Themes—most cozy mysteries have some kind of theme (cooking, clocks, yard sales, apples, farming, etc.) that have to be incorporated into the story. One of the reasons people read a specific book is because of the theme. As a writer I must balance using enough of the theme to make the reader happy while not letting the theme overwhelm the story and keep the protagonist from solving the mystery. One of the many things I love about cozies is that there are all different themes. Cate Conte writes a paranormal series; Jessica Ellicott a historical series set between World War I and II; there are numerous culinary series like Olivia Matthews' Spice Island Bakery mysteries. V.M. Burns writes the dog club and bookshop mysteries, among others. There is truly something for everyone.

Methods of killing people—cozy villains usually don't have guns, knives, or bombs. They kill with household items—a common poison (no biological weapons stolen from a super-secret facility), pitchforks, picture frames. Cozy writers have to be very creative to stay within the expectations of their readers and come up with unique way to kill someone. In a cozy you won't ever see the murder through the eyes of the killer. The cozy protagonist will stumble upon the body or have a friend find the body.

The investigation—no one is going to call a cozy protagonist and say, "Sarah, we've got a situation and you're the only person who can solve this crime." More often than not, a cozy protagonist is being told to stay out of the investigation. They don't have access to crime scene photos, DNA evidence from the scene, or autopsy results that might help their investigation. Cozy writers must get creative so that it's somewhat plausible (and we trust that our readers will allow us a little leeway) that an amateur sleuth can solve a crime.

Cozy protagonists rely on their knowledge of the community they live in, their relationships with people, their ability to suss out liars, and their keen observational skills to solve the mystery. Convincing the reader to look one way while playing fair with the clues is what makes writing a cozy so difficult and what makes reading one so satisfying.

Cozy mysteries don't need defense, they need respect.

NOTES

1. The good news is in 2022 Mystery Writers of America announced a new Edgar® Award called the Lilian Jackson Braun Award. It includes a $2000 prize to the author of a cozy mystery. Additionally, for years the Malice Domestic conference sponsors the Agatha Awards that focus on cozy and traditional mysteries.

2. Sandra Jackson-Opoku was one of the Sisters in Crime Academic Grant Reports recipients in 2021, and spoke at How SinC Changed My Life: Hearing from SinC Award Winners, Celebrate SinC 35, 9/24/2022.

Why I Became a Cozy Writer—
And Why I'm Happy I Did

Vicki Delany

I am now the author of five (yes, five) cozy mystery series, with three publishers, under two names.

I started my writing career writing standalone novels of psychological suspense, what's now so hugely popular under the label of domestic suspense, all with a dual story line in which something that happened in the past is affecting people in the present and the problem of the past must be resolved so the present-day people can get on with their lives. I then wrote an eight-book police procedural series set in a small town in British Columbia, Canada. In between those, I wrote a series of four books set in the Yukon in 1898, at the heart of the Klondike Gold Rush, and seven novellas.

None of these books were "graphic" or gory in any way, but the violence, the threat of violence, and remembered violence were ever-present. The crimes were dark and often disturbing as could be with what else was going on in people's lives: missing parents, runaway children, suicidal ex-soldiers, shunned lovers out for revenge, serial killers, terrorism. Whether police doing what police do, or people caught up in events out of their control, they had difficult things to deal with. Sometimes the protagonists succeeded, and sometimes they did not.

In all of my books the fallout of the murder or crime is widespread and devastating. In one book, my police officer protagonist kills a man. I dealt with the murder of a mother, the disappearance of a father, the suspected betrayal of a spouse, the death of adult children (not touching little kids), a man who went to prison for twenty-five years for a crime he didn't commit, and an ex-soldier with PTSD and a gun on his lap. The standalones were about dysfunctional families and the lasting repercussions of wartime trauma. I completed a book (never published) about a tough-as-they-come former cop whose niece is sold to a sex-trafficking ring and sets out to find her.

> *"When I decided to become a police officer I knew I'd have to deal with the hard side of life. Beaten children, raped women, accident victims, blood and gore. But that's not the hardest part, is it? It's the goddamn tragedy of peoples' lives."*
>
> —Constable Molly Smith to Sergeant John Winters,
> *Among the Departed* by Vicki Delany

Then, about six years ago, I was starting to get a bit, shall we say, burned out? I was seriously thinking about giving up writing. I can't really say why; maybe I wasn't having fun with it anymore. Tough stuff, even fictionally, is tough to deal with sometimes.

I had a vague idea for a new standalone, maybe something about a World War II–era ghost living in an abandoned barn that's being developed for a new winery, which wasn't going anywhere, when I was asked by Kim Lionetti of Bookends Literary Agency if I'd like to try my hand at the Lighthouse Library series work-for-hire Berkley was offering.

Sure, thought I. Might as well. I gave it a go, got the contract, and I've never looked back. I am now writing the eleventh Lighthouse Library mystery.

Fast forward a few years and I write five cozy mystery series totaling, to date, more than thirty books. The darker stuff has been left far behind. After putting in my time writing police procedurals and psychological thrillers, I'm having a lot of fun writing cozies. Keep it light, keep it funny, and have a good time with it.

Before I go on, I should explain what a cozy mystery means—as I see it, anyway. Cozies are often described as having no graphic sex or violence, which is true, but you can have a highly dark and disturbing novel that has no graphic sex or violence but is psychologically grim.

To me the essence of a cozy is that there is no sense of tragedy, as discussed in the quote from *Among the Departed*, above. (Occasionally, the protagonist will have experienced tragedy in the past, which has caused her to move to a new community or return to an old one.) People in cozies do not live tragic lives and they don't fear tragic happenings. Someone is murdered, and that's never funny, but they are generally not much liked by the community or are strangers to it. Their death needs to be solved so that the perfect, orderly community can go back to the way it was—perfect and orderly. The characters live in an essentially good world that needs to be put back to rights. The problems they encounter in their lives—other than the murder—are the sort of things we all deal with: antagonistic co-workers, demanding relatives, romantic rivals, the neighbor who puts up an ugly fence on the property line or doesn't bring their trash containers in. No human trafficking rings, child prostitutes, mob hit men, domestic terrorists, or Russian assassins here.

The cozy mystery is set in a nice, pleasant place. The sort of town you'd like to live in. The characters are, generally, nice people. They might have their differences, but the protagonist usually has a circle of friends and coworkers who are always on her side. The murder interrupts the peace of this pleasant community, and it is up to the protagonist to put things back to rights. The murder is solved, the criminal is apprehended, justice is done, and the community returns to being a nice place to live.

It may sound formulaic, and it is, but the secret of a good formula is what you do with it.

A cozy mystery is, almost always, a genuine puzzle mystery, meaning a game of wits between the author and the reader. The clues are laid out in such a way that the astute reader has a chance of solving the mystery immediately before or at the same time the protagonist does. The author has the daunting task of presenting the story in such a way that the clues are not obvious and muddying the waters by laying a suitable number of red herrings and false trails. Of course, the red herrings and false trails can't look like red herrings and false trails on first reading! But the author must at all times "play fair." The clues to the mystery need to be presented clearly and in such a way that, on a second reading, the reader cries, "Of course!"

What distinguishes a cozy mystery from a traditional mystery that might also be a puzzle mystery is what we call the hook. Cozy mysteries focus on a theme of the character's job or hobby. Bakery owner, restauranteur, librarian, bookstore owner, dance instructor, book binder, jewelry maker, the list is almost endless. This hook must feature in the book. Readers want to know more about this job or hobby. In my Sherlock Holmes Bookshop series, all the books and merchandise sold in the fictional store exist in the real world. In my Tea by the Sea books, teatime recipes are provided.

Real people, real things. Another feature of cozy mysteries is that that they are life writ large. Everything is exaggerated. The nosy neighbor is nosier, the ditzy friend is ditsier, the mean girl is meaner. And the handsome man is, well, handsomer. Even better if there are two of them.

Sounds a bit silly? Sure it does. And it's supposed to be. It's nothing but fun, and what's wrong with that?

Cozy novels are often disparaged as being fluff or unrealistic, not serious. (*I mean, books that include recipes?*) But I get a great deal of mail from readers telling me that that's what they want in a book. Particularly over the pandemic, people wrote to me about how they were so tired and depressed watching the news or reading books in which bad things happen to good people. They told me they want to escape into cozies; they enjoy visiting a world in which there are good people, doing good things, and having happy endings.

Cozies are often mocked for being unrealistic, but let's face it: most genre fiction relies on over-dramatization and coincidence, on people remembering and noticing things that normal people are too pre-occupied with their lives do.

I see an additional element to the disparagement of cozies. They are almost exclusively written by women and about women. (Although there are some exceptions.) Are women's lives and women's work still not taken entirely seriously? Think about what I consider the male fantasy novel: the rogue CIA agent who with the help of the beautiful Russian spy saves civilization as we know it, or the average hapless guy who, with the help of the beautiful, mysterious stranger, saves civilization as we know it (or at least his small part of it).

Between cozies and the male fantasy novel, I know which is more realistic to me.

Even gritty police detective novels rely on a lot of unrealism. Very few cops encounter master criminals in their time, and most police work (as police officers have told me) is boring and repetitive. Particularly in a small town they often know who did it before even investigating. As a cop once said to me: "If they weren't morons, we wouldn't catch half of them."

The cozy protagonist solves crimes though her intelligence and wits and her observation of people's behavior. She has no forensic evidence to ponder or legal resources to consult. She can't even make people talk to her if they don't want to. She solves crimes without the use of violence, but she will fight when necessary to defend herself and others.

The cozy heroine is never a renegade, never a loner. She might have conflicts with other people, often with the police, but she relies on her friends and her colleagues, her team, to have her back and work with her. A cozy mystery is often about teamwork. People work together for a common good rather than at odds, as is the situation in so many "tough guy" police or PI books. In many cozy books the police are either incompetent or untrustworthy. I've tried hard not to do that. In all my cozies, the amateur sleuth works with the police detectives and (after some initial conflict and suspicion) they begin to trust her instincts. Sound unrealistic? Sure it is, but see above about the "male fantasy novel."

One hitch in writing books in which the character deduces the solution to the crime by observation of human nature: you can't take that to court! As an extra twist in a modern cozy novel, the observation and deductions must be backed up by evidence. Even a dramatic confession on the part of the guilty person (so beloved of Golden Age mysteries) is likely to be thrown out of court. To this end my protagonist and the police have to work together—she tells them what might have happened or what likely happened. And they get the proof they need.

Again—teamwork!

For me, as a writer, I've found since I switched from darker novels to cozies that writing can be fun again. I love writing cozies. I have three or four books published each year. I approach every day (well, almost every day) excited to get back to the computer and into the story.

The word I often use for the cozies I write is *fun*. They should be fun for the author and fun for the reader. Not all cozies are humorous, but I hope mine are. Writing humor, I've found, makes me smile. Maybe I was burning out with the stuff I was writing, but the cozies have given me a giant boost. Then again, maybe I'm just enjoying not worrying about grief, and loss, and the tragedy of human existence.

Cozies are intended to be nothing more than an entertaining read. You won't learn many lessons about the human condition; no one is suffering from angst or threating to kill themselves because of depression. No PTSD. No terrorist attacks or serial killers. Just people with friends and lovers and community. And the occasional enemy. And a murder, of course.

Cozy mysteries are not trying to make an important statement about modern society or hoping to change the world. A cozy mystery tells a story that attempts to be entertaining, that's about people much like us (or like us if we were prettier, or smarter, or younger!) and our friends and family.

Cozy mysteries are the perfect read for our troubled times.

From Following the Rules
and Regs to Throwing Them
Out the Window

Justin M. Kiska

When I sat down to write my first book, *Now & Then*, I never thought much about what mystery genre it fit into. I just knew I had an idea for an interesting story I wanted to tell. The same was true for the mysteries I used to read before I started writing. I never spent any time thinking about what *kind* of mystery they were. I believe, like a lot of mystery readers, at the end of the day, I just like a good whodunit. It wasn't until *Now & Then* was picked up for a series that I began really looking at all the various types of genres and started thinking about where Parker City Mysteries fit on the spectrum. While the books in my series have different levels of history intertwined in the narrative, as well as a dual timeline to the story, and a touch of humor, they are unquestionably police procedurals.

Mystery genres, just like all literary genres at this point, are no longer as cut and dried as they used to be. There are so many different subgenres and crossover genres. Just walk into a bookstore that really takes the time to classify their offerings. Plus, there are those readers and reviewers who don't agree on what books fit into which genre.

I once read a review for a great mystery where the reviewer was complaining that the book was a Young Adult novel and they never would have read it if they'd known it was YA. Their reasoning behind calling it YA was one of the main characters whose point of view we saw on and off throughout the book was a teenager. Never once when I was reading the book did I think it would be classified as YA. There were quite a few events and situations that would never be in a YA book. And the teenager was only one of many characters—all of which were adults. After I read the offending review, I turned to my wife and said that by this reviewer's standards,

Stephen King's *It* is a Young Adult novel just because the main characters are children. I've never met anyone who thinks *It* should be shelved alongside Percy Jackson. But I digress.

Someone at a book club once asked me how I would describe my mysteries to a person who'd never read them. After thinking about it for a minute, I told them—and have since continued to say—I would equate my books to having the feel of the '80s cop television shows created by Stephen J. Cannell. They're lightly gritty with a little bit of humor and not too violent.

So, if I write police procedurals, why, then, you may be asking yourself at this moment, am I writing a piece for a collection about cozy mysteries. The answer to this is because I have been developing a new series—at least I hope it turns into a series—that fits squarely into the cozy genre. It will be a complete departure from my first books. Don't get me wrong. If I had to choose, I would say police procedurals are my favorite type of mystery, and I fully expect to continue writing in that vein in the future. But there is something pulling at me to step away from the rigid structure of a police investigation and the rules that go along with it for a little while and try something different.

What's the difference going to be for me writing a cozy mystery versus a police procedural? First, the level of humor. Even though I always include some lighthearted moments in my books between the detectives—after all, even in the most stressful of situations people turn to humor as a defense mechanism—overall, the police procedural genre is not known for its comedic works. That doesn't mean they don't exist. It's just not what readers are expecting when they pick up a book in Michael Connelly's Harry Bosch or Louise Penny's Armand Gamache series. Cozy mysteries, however, are much more suited to moments of humor and irreverent situations. Just by the sheer fact that the "detective" in the majority of cozies is not a member of law enforcement in any way, shape, or form and yet they are trying to solve a murder or catch a criminal makes them much less realistic and more appropriate for amusing antics. From priests to librarians to cooks, in a cozy mystery anyone can solve a crime. Not to mention all the pets out there solving crimes. In the real world, if you were a florist who kept sticking your nose into a murder investigation, you'd be locked up for obstruction of justice. And if I were writing one of my police procedurals and a florist kept getting in the way of my detectives, that's exactly what I would have to have them do to said investigation interloper.

No matter how much you love Jessica Fletcher—and I do—there would have been no way she would have been able to get away with even a fraction of what she did in a realistic mystery series. Yet, in a cozy series, the everyday person is *expected* to be the crime solver. Which is why, in a new cozy mystery series, I will have some more freedom to allow my "detectives" to get themselves into situations normal people wouldn't find themselves. The words *shenanigans* and *high jinx* keep coming to mind. From funny one-liners in the dialogue to characters finding themselves in these crazy, mad-cap circumstances, I'm ready to write a more humorous mystery for readers where a good joke doesn't have to be disregarded because if a police officer said it at a crime scene it would be completely inappropriate. But if an amateur sleuth says it, it gets a laugh.

Writing a cozy will also be nice because it will give me a chance to break away from the built-in structure that naturally comes with a police procedural. Let's face it, it's in the title … police *procedural*. Any good author who writes about a police force, whether real or fictional, needs to follow set rules, regulations, and … yes … procedures in their mysteries. Authors who desire a strong sense of reality really lean into the techniques and practices used by law enforcement. And we certainly see an audience for these types of mysteries just by looking at the television guide and seeing all the police procedurals being offered, though some would argue these shows don't always get it right. But that's for the experts to debate.

Whether in a book or on television, the investigators in a police procedural are still tied to a set of rules that must be followed—however loosely. Some would argue that it is because of these types of books (and television shows) that people know so much of what they know about the Miranda Warning, search warrants, and interrogation techniques. There can be some literary license taken at times, true, but at the heart of it, these are all real, indelible aspects of our justice system that authors must contend with and address if they are writing a reality-based mystery.

Cozies, on the other hand, don't necessarily need to worry about one's Constitutional rights, and for the most part, their readers aren't expecting it. One of the best examples I can think of is if a police officer knows a suspect is hiding evidence in his or her office and is afraid they are going to destroy it. If the author is trying to adhere to any semblance of reality—and doesn't want their detective to be one of those cops that throws the rule book out the window because the ends justify the means—they would need to have their investigator go through the proper channels and follow the rules to obtain a search warrant. In the real world, this could take more than enough time for the suspect to dispose of the evidence and get away with the crime. In a novel, the author can—if he or she desires—just make a passing reference to having obtained a search warrant without going into much detail and all is well. But there is still the need to think about it.

In a cozy mystery, our intrepid florist could create a beautiful bouquet of flowers and deliver them to the suspect's office and, while there, snoop around, find the evidence they are looking for, and take it. No search warrant needed. For the sake of this essay, let's set aside the issues of potential trespassing, burglary, and obstruction of justice. The florist always gets their man!

After years of researching police procedures, crime scene protocols, and the way the legal system operates in the state in which my novels take place—not to mention how things were done differently during the various historic time periods I've written about—it will be nice to not have to think so much about that. By nature, I am a rule follower. But I find in my writing, on occasion, they can be constraining. In taking on a cozy mystery, my detectives will have more freedom to follow their hunches and investigate the crime the way the average person would think it should be done without being hindered by a badge and everything that comes along with wearing one.

There's one other area my new mysteries will be different from my first. The characters. In a cozy, the characters who populate the series' world have a tendency to be a little more over the top, eccentric, and "peculiar" at times. These types of characters add a fun dimension to the story. Not that you can't find a quirky character in a police procedural, but there's a better chance to find more of them in a cozy. Parker City Mysteries has its fair share of characters with unique traits that make them stand out, but I've never created a character so over the top that they are unbelievable. Character development in any literary genre is key. Whether it's a comedy or drama, mystery or romance, readers want good characters who are fleshed out and they can connect with in some way. Even if they can't *connect* with them, they understand them. Because chances are, like me, you've read a good mystery where the detective character just wasn't developed well and it brought the whole story down. But character development is a conversation for another time.

As I wrote earlier, my own preference usually runs more toward a procedural when I am looking for my next book to read. But whatever the genre, I just want a clever mystery to solve. There's nothing better than a well-thought-out whodunit? Ever since Edgar Allan Poe wrote "The Murders in the Rue Morgue," mysteries have become such a part of our entertainment culture. With each new generation of authors, the genre only gets better and better. Sir Arthur Conan Doyle and Agatha Christie gave us some of the greatest mysteries of all time. Today we have Michael Connelly and Louise Penny, two that I mentioned earlier, and James Patterson and Harlan Coben, all building off of the mystery writers who came before them.

You can see, at least in my mind, there's quite a difference between a police procedural and a cozy mystery. Procedurals are more realistic and graphic while cozies are just that, more *cozy*—much less dramatic. And as I set out to write my first cozy, I want to make it as different as possible from my first series which relies heavily on getting the facts right about how a real police investigation is conducted and what detectives must go through to solve a case. My new book is going to find my detectives in the classic small town surrounded by quirky characters finding themselves in over their heads when they decide to try and solve a murder, something neither of them would ever be expected to do. For the record, neither will be a florist and I certainly did not mean to offend any crime fighting florist with this essay.

Crimes of Fashion

Diane Vallere

I was ten years old when I discovered Trixie Belden. A friend of mine had the entire collection, and she would loan me a new book every morning after swim team practice. I'd go home and finish it that day, then return it the following day and start the next one. It was our own version of a little free library.

Ten years old was a pivotal age for me. It's also when I started a detective agency—not unrelated to my newfound love of Trixie, I'm sure. But while most Trixie fans connected to her tomboy attitude and defiance of anything "girly," I enjoyed the makeover parts too: when Trixie went shopping with her mother for a party outfit or an appropriate wardrobe for an unexpected vacation getaway with the other Bob-Whites.

Over the next years, I moved from Trixie Belden to Nancy Drew, from Nancy Drew to Connie Blair. I grew up, graduated, and went on to have a successful career in retail fashion. I never lost my love of Trixie Belden—or of mysteries. In the back of my mind, the desire to write my own children's mystery series remained. The problem that kept me from doing so was somewhat critical: I didn't have any ideas!

My two loves intersected after a career move took me from Pennsylvania to Texas and made me a fish out of water (not coincidentally my favorite type of story). I visited the public library on a lunch break and discovered the world of cozy mysteries. They were like Trixie Beldens—but for adults. Writing that sounded like a lot of fun.

Shortly thereafter, my idea for a mystery followed: a fashion buyer who gives up her glamorous career and takes a job in the town where she grew up—and discovers her new boss dead in an elevator on her first day on the job.

This is the concept for *Designer Dirty Laundry*, my first book. Fun fact: at the time, I always had anxiety about flying, but my job had me on a plane every other month. I started using that time to write. I wrote about Samantha Kidd on airplanes while flying from Texas to the locales where my job took me—New York, Milan, and Paris—further intertwining the concepts of fashion and mysteries in my mind. (I quickly learned that those concepts were not intertwined with my coworkers who could talk about fashion for hours but did *not* share my interest in murder.)

I found writing about Samantha Kidd in that first book to be easy. I gave her a degree in the history of fashion, a college major that sounds fabulous to me, and gives her the added benefit of being able to look at clothes and see something in addition to the color or cut. (I was an art history major, so I like to imagine it's just like that but with clothes instead of paintings), and I gave her my career as a shoe buyer, which I knew was both creative and analytical. These skills serve her well even though she doesn't have a clue how to solve a mystery!

Common writing advice is to write what you know, and not only did I know her world, but I also knew her exact situation: having a job that most people would find enviable but recognizing that it didn't make her happy. I understood wanting to take a few steps backward and figure out what it is that will. I put Samantha into a situation where she was destined to fail—wrong place, wrong time; killer actively framing her—and I armed her with what she thought was the most important thing she had: her extensive wardrobe. By the end of the book, after being literally stripped bare, she realizes it's not her clothes that make her who she is, it's what is underneath: her resilience.

But a funny thing happened after I got that first idea. I was still working in retail at the time, and suddenly every day, everywhere I looked, I saw opportunities for mysteries. Unpacking a trunk of samples? What if there was a body underneath the clothes? Or hidden in the walk-in steamer?

I saw motives for murder, too. Pressures to meet sales quotas, cutthroat commission dynamics, overbearing managers, embezzling schemes. I recognized how many situations could easily lead to mysteries in the fashion or fashion-adjacent industry. I'd gone from wanting to write but not having any ideas to having so many ideas I needed to quit my job to have enough time to write them.

It shouldn't have surprised me that a mystery series about fashion was never really about fashion. I did what the advice books say, and I wrote what I knew. And because my introduction to mysteries had been through series, after finishing that first book, I started to write Samantha's next mystery, and then the next one after that. Each book centered on a different fashionable mystery, and each time Samantha learned a little bit more about herself and got further along in her quest for happiness.

Samantha's first attempt at a fresh start doesn't work out the way she wants, but she's not willing to give up on her new life. In book two, she takes a job at a hot new retailer, only to discover it's not her resume that makes them hire her but her experience uncovering a murderer. Book three places her in a volunteer role helping her friend curate a fashion exhibit at the local museum, and book four puts her in charge of a runway show that goes off the rails. Book five features a long-lost sample collection from the seventies, and book six features a jewelry sales rep and an outlet mall at the holidays. Book seven brings the mafia who, it turns out, have an investment claim on a shoe design business, and book eight goes to Las Vegas for the lingerie market. In book nine, there's a new British owner of the department store where Samantha started out in book one, and in book ten, she's living life as a fashion influencer.

Book eleven—inspired by the podcast *Serial*—is one of my favorites in the series. It features a former magazine editor and classmate of Samantha's serving a life sentence for a crime she claims she did not commit. Book twelve is all about jeans, book thirteen has a trunk of mod memorabilia purchased at auction, and book fourteen is set at a fashion awards ceremony. After a recent binge of *Yellowstone*, I wanted to send Samantha off to a dude ranch, so book fifteen features western wear (also a bit of an inside joke on the series since Samantha makes a disparaging internal comment about western style in book one. Plus, the horsey setting allowed me to lean on what I learned from Trixie Belden all those years ago!). I've got three ideas on deck for future books. In terms of source material, fashion as a backdrop has paid off in dividends.

After I wrote a few Samantha Kidd books, I had an idea for another character, this one an interior decorator who modeled her life after Doris Day. I wanted her to be completely different from Samantha, so I dressed her in vintage—but not good vintage: double-knit polyester ensembles she acquires by default after buying out estates rich in original mid-century modern pieces. She wears Keds every day because she sustained a knee injury, and heels are out of the picture. She lives in Texas (where she moved from Pennsylvania—*write what you know*) and works for herself. Opposite, right? Apparently not. Madison Night, my new sleuth, used her personal style as much as Samantha did. She is a walking business card for her decorating company. In a world of yoga pants and cargo shorts, Madison dressed like an extra from *Pillow Talk*. Her style says a lot about her willingness to ignore convention and be her own person. Even my editor told me part of the fun of the series is reading about her kooky vintage ensembles.

My third series featured a fashion school graduate who, before inheriting a fabric store, oversaw a pageant dress workshop and adopted a wardrobe of black every day to hide dirt and grime (but loves, collects, and deconstructs vintage gowns from the thirties in her spare time).

My fourth series features a woman raised by a single father who owned a costume shop with his wife before she died. Overwhelmed with grief, he dressed their daughter in costumes from his store, establishing a unique style she maintains as an adult—now helping him run the store.

Even when I went to outer space in my fifth series, I wrote about the uniform a lieutenant wore on a spaceship. By book three, she's wear-testing prototype uniforms, and in book four she's the sales rep.

Working in the fashion industry gave me an insider's view, but there's no doubt that I've surpassed my firsthand experience and now conduct significant research for each book. The same love of fashion that landed me my first job, selling sneakers at a department store before going on to be the buyer of designer shoes at a luxury retailer, is what sustains me now as a mystery author.

What is it about fashion that lends itself so well to multiple series? For starters, it's a multi-billion-dollar industry that includes more than a dozen touches before the merchandise ever lands in a store: design, development, vendor compliance, material sourcing, factory sourcing, manufacturing, shipping, consolidation, customs clearance, wholesale. Then there's the buying process: showroom employees, retail buyers, warehousing, and ground transportation. A store needs a manager and employees (and an advertising team behind the scenes). The *business* of fashion is filled with possibilities—each one with potential for a mystery.

And then there's personal style, the shorthand that transmits our identities to the world. You may argue that your cozy sweats don't capture the nuance that is your multidimensional personality, but those cozy sweats are still your choice. There's a reason human resource departments advise employees to dress for the job they want, not the job they have. Those wardrobe choices tell the higher-ups to notice employees who are eager for advancement.

Characters can project who they are through their clothing choices, but they're also able to hide behind styles that *aren't* their usual choice.

Mysteries all start with a what-if and fashionable mysteries are no different. What if a person dresses like they're something they're not? What if a person is found wearing something they normally wouldn't be caught dead in? What if a uniform eliminates the possibility of judging a person based on their outfit? What if a person must get lost in a crowd and adopt a quickie disguise? What if someone with unique style must suddenly fit in to be considered credible? What if someone's signature look is what links them to a crime scene?

Clothes, they say, make the man, but they also make the woman, the victim, the killer, and the suspects. Clothing choices say a lot about each of us, and for a person versed in the language of fashion, it's easy to make (sometimes erroneous) decisions based on those choices. Samantha Kidd spent her career in a job where how people dressed indicated their level of success, a lesson that doesn't always pan out in terms of identifying people with suspicious motives. It becomes one more lesson to for her to learn on her journey to uncover the truth of her new boss's murder.

Now, when I have an idea for a new series, one of the first things I do is imagine my character's style. On deck are a coroner who wears her deceased father's collection of vintage Philadelphia sports jerseys and an unlikely fixer who wears track suits and collects sneakers. Once I can "see" them, there's a better chance they'll get their own book.

When I set out to write a mystery, I didn't plan to make everything I wrote connect back to the world of fashion and style. At first, I was surprised when reviews called that my hallmark. Eventually, I leaned into it. Fashion has been blamed for creating unrealistic beauty standards, encouraging street crimes, and tempting criminals with opportunities to steal, knock off, and embezzle. Clothes are the easiest way to make us look like something we're not, and that's extra valuable when trying to either skulk about looking for clues or get away with a crime!

Where Subgenres Overlap

Kait Carson

Is it a cozy or a traditional mystery? Does it really matter?

In truth, all cozies are traditional mysteries, but not all traditional mysteries are cozy. It's a matter of nuance, voice, and writing style. Therein lies the rub. The first mysteries I read were written by the marvelous Brits. Daphne du Maurier, P.D. James, and Mary Stewart, followed in quick succession by Agatha Christie, Ruth Rendell, and Marian Babson (although she was an American by birth). I also read Phyllis Whitney (born in Japan to American parents). There was no distinction made at the time between cozy and traditional; the books were simply mysteries. I steeped myself in the small towns and craved to discover what a stile looked like in real life. If I ever saw one, I'd be looking for a body on the other side. One that looked peaceful, as if it was sleeping, not covered in bloody stains. The concept of an unnatural peaceful death tweaked my imagination. So did the broader concept of emotional death. There is more than one way to kill a victim.

As a practicing paralegal with a probate and estates practice that included litigation, I'd seen more than my fair share of "he done me wrong" court cases. Most often those were civil suits. A few in the realm of criminal courts. The things greedy and desperate relatives get up to when they think no one is looking would curdle your blood. It served as a good introduction to the ways and means of killing people without shedding blood. There's an oft quoted cliché that's been attributed to authors from Twain to Hemingway: Write what you know. This is what I know: the seven deadly sins are real and present in the twenty-first century. I'd seen them in action. And they can be deadly, in a genteel, bloodless way.

When I decided to write, I turned to the mysteries that were my catnip. Spiraling themes and dark nights of the soul all called to me. My heroines lived in small town tropical or rural settings. They drank wine and ate health food, made healthy lifestyle choices. Their hobbies were running and scuba diving. None frequented smoke-filled rooms, bars smelling of stale beer and spilled scotch, or rat-infested alleys inhabited by gun-toting good or evil doers. Even my proposed villains led everyday lives. They resided in the same small towns as my sleuths. Oftentimes I envisioned them as people known and trusted in the community and by my heroines.

Chipping away the veneer of civility and exposing not the dark underbelly but the chinks in the armor attracted me. In my first book, my heroine, Catherine Swope, had been a cop, her career derailed when she shot a teen in self-defense. Despite internal affairs calling it a good shoot, Catherine couldn't forgive herself. She spiraled into a haze of wine and self-recrimination and only emerged as, of all things, a dog-walker. She had always been an animal lover, and critters paved her road to redemption. Much of this sounds as if it would be a dark mystery, but little of the backstory, and none of the violence, appears on the page. The book and the story concentrate on Catherine's investigation, her relationships, and, ultimately, her redemption.

The villain in this book is a well-respected man who leads a double life, one of service and self-service. In the end, protecting his secrets is more important to him than taking the moral high road. He kills and, in his arrogance, believes he can get away with it. He almost does.

Does this sound like a dark story? It's not, not in the reading, but despite having the tropes of a cozy mystery, an amateur sleuth (albeit a former cop), a devoted dog and cat, a sidekick friend, a cop boyfriend, a small-town setting, no violence on the page, and certainly no sex or blue language, it's a traditional mystery. The theme of the book is betrayal, there are few light-hearted or comedic moments, neither the dog nor the cat talk, and no one cooks. Because of the protagonist's background and her close personal relationship with a police officer, the book borders on the police procedural genre. The investigative steps develop the story. Coincidences are few and far between.

When I sat down to write this book, I planned a cozy. My reading hours were spent curled up with cozies. Lilian Jackson Braun's *The Cat Who* series saw me through the recovery period from major surgery. I lived in a small town populated by everyday people. Okay, one of those everyday people was a former Watergate burglar. He'd done his time and his kids had a garage band. Couldn't get more "cozy" than that. The setting for the first Swope book was my small town. Fictionalized, of course. Cozies, to me, were tomato soup and grilled cheese. Comfort food for the tired soul. Bad things happened, but they came right in the end. And there was hope. Always hope. I couldn't imagine writing in any other genre, nor did I want to.

As the writing progressed, it became clear that Catherine wasn't comfortable with the light-hearted, easy-reading style of a cozy. Perhaps because she'd been a cop. Someone who saw the dark underbelly of humanity. She insisted on harder edges and more realistic description. Justice would prevail, but it would come at an uncomfortable cost. She railed against the softening of reality. Death wasn't pretty. Not in the real world, not in Catherine's world. For every ten words I wrote in the soft, cozy style, five fell victim to the delete key. As a writer, if I've learned anything, it's to listen to your characters. They know more than I do, and if I'm lucky, they'll share their knowledge. Catherine spoke, and I followed her lead. My cozy lost its light edge and ventured into a traditional mystery. The tone, the depth of the investigation, and the overall theme of the book required a move out of the cozy realm.

Despite it all, the cozy genre still called to me. I was determined to crack the code. My second series sold to a well-known cozy mystery publisher. I was thrilled. Until the publisher made it clear that the series was meant to be a part of their traditional mystery offerings. In retrospect, that was probably pre-destined. My protagonist is a paralegal and the publishing house was in the process of branching out from comic cozies to darker fare. Hayden Kent couldn't cook and her life was defined by statutes and pleadings. It was natural for her to use professional-level research skills to uncover clues. Even the introduction of her scuba diving hobby to further the investigation wasn't sufficient to lighten the book to a cozy level.

Thoroughly frustrated by my failure to write what I loved, I dug deeper into researching the bones of the genre. Cozies and lighter traditionals intersect at almost every point. Although some traditional mysteries include professional sleuths, urban locations, violence on the page, sex, and cussing, I had been careful to exclude these options from my works. So what was I missing? It wasn't recipes. My books didn't pretend to be culinary mysteries and not all cozies feature recipes or chefs.

To find the answer, I did what any writer does. I wrote another book. This one was set in the Florida Keys, featured a millennial heroine with three sidekicks, a police officer boyfriend, and humor. It took place during the famous Key West Fantasy Fest, replete with tropical drinks, sandy beaches, and, of course, murder. Certain of my craft points, I sent the book out to my beta reader. Hoping to discover the secret handshake, I selected as my betas for this book cozy writers who both wrote cozies and whose opinions I trusted. The response: great book, fun read, but it's not a cozy. Pro tip. If you're going to be a writer, develop a tribe that includes honest and open fellow writers. A thick skin doesn't hurt, either.

I knew there were borderline traditional scenes. The story dealt with drugs (it's Florida) and drinking (it's Key West). I expected suggestions to tone those scenes down and the story would be good to go. Instead, suggestions were made to develop more of the tropical sensory material—the rub of sand under bare feet, the taste of tropical air before a storm, the chatter of parrots in trees, the scalding pain of a sunburn—and to make more use of the main character's pet. I'd mentioned each of these items in the story, but I hadn't featured the setting as a character to the extent that a cozy demands. I'd also failed to make good use of the cat. Hank's cat served as a lap ornament rather than a plot device. Strange, because I'm a cat owner, and my four would revolt if that was the only attention they received.

I returned to the story and critically read each line. The aim wasn't to pad the words, although it did increase the word count. Instead, it was to take the descriptive sentences and use them to send the reader on vacation. Cozy settings can be locked rooms, street festivals, tropical beaches, or double black diamond ski slopes. Small towns, a place where everyone knows everyone, or at least the people who matter to the story, are featured. The place isn't as important as establishing that the crime is an aberration, order is restored, and, in the end, the setting becomes safe again. The hard edges of reality were removed, and the action takes place behind a gossamer scrim. The book is now pending review with the cozy imprint of a "big five" publisher and I have my fingers crossed.

Certain now of my cozy chops, I undertook to start a new series. This one based in my birth state of New Jersey. Despite my being ever mindful of the crossroads of cozy and traditional, my beta readers and editor tell me that, although the book has cozy elements, it's traditional. Again, no violence takes place on the page, but there are several deaths, murders, in fact, and the tension level is ratcheted beyond that of a cozy. The amateur sleuth and posse of friends conventions are honored, but my sleuth actively investigates and develops clues apart from the very competent police investigator with whom she shares her insights and theories. Worse, there's a love interest in this book that teeters on the brink of making it a romantic suspense. My betas suggested pursuing this relationship and broadening the genre of the book. And here I was even considering including a recipe or two.

My research makes it clear that there is a distinct difference between the cozy and the traditional mystery, and any number of books, blog posts, and essays are available to define the process for each. These may be helpful for some writers. Two years of try/fail have taught me that I am not one of those writers. Instead, my process is to write mysteries that pique my interest in a linear and realistic way. My voice tends to realism with a hint of hard edge rather than humor. In short, it's time to accept that I am not a cozy writer. Not on the first or second draft. Cozy comes to me only through extensive re-writes, and the effort comes across on the page. My natural voice is traditional. The lack of graphic content gives it a cozy edge, but that is far different from writing a cozy.

Accepting this realization has set me free. I came to the intersection of cozy and traditional, and I took the road that is more comfortable. Writing will never be an easy pursuit. It's long hours before a computer or with pen in hand. It's hours of rewriting and polishing, it's nights of angst and days of celebration. It's the best job in the world once you find, and follow, your voice. I plan to feature location-specific recipes on my webpage. Tropical foods and drinks are too tasty not to share, but they don't belong in my books. I've moved to the darker side. The place I feel most at home.

Cozy and Not-So-Cozy Novels

Defying a Sub-Genre Label

Tina deBellegarde

Many books defy categorization no matter how much our agents and editors want to pigeon-hole them. Defining a cozy mystery may seem straightforward at first, but my experience has proven just the opposite. Plenty of books meet many of the criteria of the cozy while not claiming to be one at all. Also, I have read books labeled cozies that don't meet all the criteria either. Is the problem with the labeling? The definition, as well as the evolution and perception, of the cozy all influence which books are categorized as such. It is at the very least imprecise and at most an unnecessary constraint on a writer's creative process.

I write a series some reviewers have called cozy and some have called not-so-cozy cozy. Still other reviewers are absolutely sure my books are not cozies at all. In some instances, not all, my publisher has used "cozy" as an Amazon keyword.

Why all the confusion? Could it be because the labeling of books is generally too reductive, especially when it comes to this particular sub-genre?

For me, it all started when I was writing my first book. It was a mystery, that much I knew. But I needed to identify the sub-genre, which, I was told, is a necessary piece of information to pitch a book and a series. At that time, I had never heard of the label "cozy." My initial research led me to believe that my book fell in that category: it was clean with no violence, no vulgar language, and no sex. To seal the deal, cozies are often set in a small community with a female amateur sleuth at the center of the story. Eureka! I was writing a cozy!

Shortly after this revelation, I read an article proclaiming the death of cozies. This was terribly disappointing, but I persisted in my writing. I had come too far to stop now. Then I discovered Louise Penny's books and realized that she was a kindred spirit, that my approach to writing was similar to hers. If Louise Penny's type of book had an audience, perhaps my book would as well. I decided that whatever her books were labeled, my books should be as well. The articles I read at that time described her as a cozy writer, so, I decided, cozies weren't dead and I merrily kept on writing.

I started to attend conferences in order to meet authors and agents, to take workshops, and, of course, to get my manuscript critiqued. I was told that I was not writing a cozy series and neither was Louise Penny. I continued researching her and realized that she and her publisher were not embracing the cozy label either. My confusion deepened.

I went on to learn that cozies also have other distinguishing characteristics. They have cute, illustrated covers—often including a cat or dog. The story frequently centers on a hobby or small business, and their titles routinely incorporate puns. I also learned that cozies are considered light reading and tend to the comedic with many eccentric characters. Penny's books are not light reading and they certainly tackle heavy issues. I'd like to think that my books will ask readers to reflect as well. Penny has a couple of eccentric characters, as do I, as most towns do, but our books are not over-populated with them either. Using these criteria, neither my books, nor Penny's books, qualify.

As I inched farther away from the cozy label, my head was spinning.

Just when I thought I was starting to get a handle on this problem, I read a few novels that were clearly marketed as cozies, and I realized that some *are* light. These also met all the other criteria: off-stage murder, female amateur sleuth, small community that worked together, and everyone all lived more or less happily ever after (except the murderer and the victim, of course).

But as I continued my reading, I found others more perplexing. Take, for example, Barbara Ross's Maine Clambake series. If I had read *Clammed Up* without the cover, I might not have considered it a cozy. Ross tackles complex relational and community problems. This book is serious and wonderful—not funny, not cute. It is heart-warming, justice prevails and you want to escape to the community, but it is not unsubstantial. The publisher's decision to go "cozy" is on the surface only. There is little difference between my books and Ross's books except for the covers and titles.

Laura Jensen Walker's heroine in *Murder Most Sweet*, billed as a cozy, is a breast cancer survivor who chooses to go flat and not have reconstructive surgery. Walker's books are also fun and warm, but we must admit that Walker tackles at least one very difficult issue head-on.

And then there's Martha Grimes. Her Richard Jury series is what hooked me into the mystery genre and is what I aspired to do when writing my books. As a reader (and a novice author who was merely dabbling at the time) I didn't know what her sub-genre was, and I did not care. I just enjoyed her books. Once I started writing and researching the sub-genres, I assumed she was a cozy author. Once again, no gore, no violence, no vulgarity, no sex.

The resolution on this subject came when I realized that essential to a cozy are the interpersonal relationships. If we look past the covers, puny titles, the cute cats and the crafts, we will notice that crucial to the cozy is the community. Cozies are character driven. Our characters evolve, grow. Non-cozy mysteries are generally plot driven.

So much so that my initial encounter with this problem was at a my very first conference where I attended a workshop. I sat in the back of the room since I only had a third of my manuscript written, and I was suffering from a serious bout of imposter syndrome. The first thing out of the instructor's mouth was a question: What drives a mystery novel? It was common knowledge to everyone in the room but me that mysteries were plot driven. That was a bad moment, because I knew my book was character driven. My protagonist and all her sidekicks in the tiny village were the motor behind my story. How they interacted and their individual desires, aspirations, fears, and shortcomings were what made my story tick. But it was also definitely a mystery. So how could I square this circle?

Both Penny's series and Grimes's series have professional detectives tasked with solving the crime. What is important, in my opinion, is that they both rely on the villagers and the insights that only a small community can provide to help solve the murder and restore peace. And it is through the eyes of the villagers that at the end we can see a new normal has been established and embraced. The villagers are not unscathed by the event; they are merely able to move forward because they have each other as a support system. Community is the heart of a cozy. Although we as readers love to participate in solving the mystery, we are reading also, if not primarily, to learn about the fates of the characters we have come to love. And under that definition Penny's Three Pines series, Grimes's Richard Jury series, and my Batavia-on-Hudson series can all be considered cozies.

To further add to the confusion of labeling, cozies are evolving. Urban settings are becoming more common, technology has entered the cozy story as well, and male protagonists are replacing the female amateur sleuths. In fact, we are seeing much more diverse protagonists in general. Another development is sub-genre blending, such as paranormal cozies.

In addition, the reception of the cozy has influenced how authors choose to label themselves. If cozies are considered light fare, not literature or at least not real crime fiction, there are authors who would resist having the label attached to their works. And there are readers who might resist picking one up. We have all heard of the romance reader who hides the bodice-ripping book cover. There are mystery readers who don't want to be caught reading a cozy with the classic cozy cover. The adorable covers, the same ones that attract some readers, put other readers off.

I have to ask: Do the labels really serve a purpose? It seems to me they help the publishers and the bookstores, but I don't think they help the author and maybe not even the reader. I am sure there are authors who are happy to have guidelines to follow, a successful formula. But I have to believe there are writers who find that labels constrain their creative process. Some authors want to write outside the guidelines but are so strongly urged not to, so much so that they feel they are putting their writing careers in danger when they do.

I think we underestimate our readers. It is shortsighted to believe they can't read a book with some cozy elements that also addresses important issues and maybe even gets a bit esoteric at times. Readers can handle all of it. Readers don't care what the books are labeled and are often unfamiliar with the labels. They like a book or they don't; they like what an author does or they don't.

I was working on this essay when Angela Lansbury died on October 11, 2022. Thinking about her most famous character, Jessica Fletcher, reminded me that now, whenever anyone asks me what a cozy is, I tell them it's *Murder, She Wrote*. It's about a small town and its amateur sleuth. It's clean, with no violence, profanity or sex. Jessica had no hard edges, and she was welcoming, as was Cabot Cove (if you don't consider your increased likelihood of being murdered there). The series was not centered on a craft or small business, and the title of the series, and the titles of the episodes, were not puny (at least not most of them). *Murder, She Wrote* had light-hearted moments but was not silly. It garnered numerous Emmy nominations and awards. It may be dated now, but it was a drama. So would you label *Murder, She Wrote* a cozy or not? I leave it up to you; you are right no matter what you decide. Which leads me once again to conclude that the labels are beside the point.

I still do not know if my books are cozies. All I know is that I love to write them and I think my readers love to read them. The standard definition is too confining for the modern cozy. Today, I choose to embrace the cozy label even if on the surface my book may not seem to be one. I am honored to write a book that readers escape to, where order is restored, where characters and their needs and those of the community take center stage.

Stepping Out of the Shadow of the Queen of Crime

MARY ANNA EVANS

When it comes to crime fiction, I will always have one foot in two worlds. I have been a crime novelist for twenty years, with a thirteen-book series of archaeological mysteries, an environmental thriller, two historical mysteries, and many mystery short stories to my credit. But I also write *about* crime fiction, publishing literary criticism that focuses on crime fiction in general and on the work of Agatha Christie in particular. I find that my academic work complements my work for a popular audience and vice versa. When I write a novel, I am conscious of the ways I am treating the topics that dominate my scholarship, particularly the question of how crime fiction deals with issues of justice; conversely, when I view someone else's work of crime fiction through a scholarly lens, I am very aware of the writing process that created the work of art I am considering. My dual experience as a mystery author and a literary scholar gives me a little glimpse behind the scenes of both fields.

If there is a downside to my dual career, it is that studying the work of Agatha Christie, the Queen of Crime, can be daunting if I allow myself to compare my own creative work to hers. For starters, nobody can touch her sales numbers. No mystery author, except perhaps Arthur Conan Doyle, is more famous, especially among the general public. While we devoted mystery readers have the names of hundreds of crime novelists at our fingertips, when others reach into their memory banks for the name of someone who writes mysteries, they overwhelmingly come up with Agatha Christie.

At times, it seems that Christie has passed from the state of being an actual human being into a state of metaphor. This can complicate something as simple as a literature survey, because a search for "Agatha Christie" on a library website will turn up unrelated books and articles that show up just because somebody wanted to give them a title that conveyed a sense of mystery. Thus, scattered among the publications that are actually useful to the Christie scholar, one will find papers like "Beyond Agatha Christie: Relationality and Critique in Anthropological Theory," which was published in 2016 in *Anthropological Theory* and offers just this sentence as the text's tenuous connection to its title: "Critique does not necessarily mean criticism, but criticism needs to rest on critique. One way to criticize is to ask: 'who's done it?'—a bit like Agatha Christie." An editorial in a 1969 issue of *The New England Journal of Medicine*, "Dish Washing à la Mode," argues for reforming unhygienic kitchen cleaning techniques, opening with this: "A recent issue of the *Practitioner* contains in its editorial section an annotation 'Death in the Kitchen.' Agatha Christie might have created the title."

Reader, let me tell you something. When I am searching the university library for publications that address Agatha Christie, I am never going to be looking for *The New England Journal of Medicine*'s thoughts on washing dishes.

In everyday speech, "Agatha Christie" equals "mystery" equals "whodunit" equals "convoluted plot." She has become an abstraction, the human face of the things she chose to write about. Unfortunately, things that are abstracted become simplified. She is the face of cozy and traditional mystery novels, as shown by the fact that the preeminent award for those styles of mystery is called the Agatha. She dominated those subgenres for decades, so this honor is well deserved, but her identification (over-identification?) with them shoves her thrillers, plays, literary novels, memoirs, stories of the supernatural, religious stories, and poetry out of the public consciousness, and I argue that compartmentalization of this kind is detrimental to our understanding of twentieth-century literature.

If you consider the 1969 date of *The New England Journal of Medicine*'s dishwashing editorial, you will see that Agatha Christie inarguably attained metaphor status long before she was even dead. You have to wonder what she thought about being the go-to symbol for puzzle plots, murder mysteries, and unnatural death. On a more personal and contemporary note, how can nonmetaphorical human beings (like me) who happen to write mysteries hope to compete with a woman who hasn't just entered the realm of the iconic but who has indeed entered the language itself?

The short answer to that question is "We can't." The long answer, the one that doesn't require mere nonmetaphorical humans to simply give up any hope of writing crime fiction, is this: "We can't avoid her shadow, but we must learn to step out of it." Agatha Christie covered a tremendous amount of fictional territory in her long career, but we live in a big world. Nobody can exhaust all of its interesting stories, so there are tales left for us to tell. Also, we have the advantage that comes with the passage of time. We can step out of Christie's shadow merely by writing a mystery that depends on artificial intelligence or on life in a world that has long since seen the end of the British Empire.

I teach aspiring novelists at the University of Oklahoma, and I always assign at least one Christie novel in my mystery writing classes. I do not assign *And Then There Were None* with the expectation that they will copy it slavishly, complete with an island setting and a cast of extremely odious characters dying, one by one. I assign it (among other reasons) so that they can experience story strategies employed by Christie and consider how those strategies might put a new slant on their own stories.

Let me say it again. I do not want my students to copy Christie. I want them to ask themselves why her stories work, so that they can translate the universal themes in her work to something that speaks to them and to those of us who live here and now.

So what can my students (and I) take from *And Then There Were None* and make new again in the twenty-first century? Well, first of all, there is no better tutor than this book when it comes to portraying unsympathetic characters. Christie gives readers an island that is overrun by terrible people. She shows us their evil cores when she reveals what unforgivable thing each of them did to earn an invitation to the deadly island—an invitation that is a death sentence. But she does more than that. She imbues dialogue that the characters themselves would consider throwaway chatter with quick reminders of exactly who these people are. A man passes off as insignificant the deaths of dozens of indigenous people whom he abandoned to die. A young man's strongest emotion about the children he mowed down with his car is frustration that he wasn't allowed to drive for a brief time as a result. A woman who threw her pregnant maid out on the street enjoys, even flaunts, her self-righteous belief that she herself is a better person than the maid because she has avoided sexual sin. Christie created people who could tell you precisely how bad they were in a single deft sentence. This is a skill that can translate into compelling twenty-first-century fiction.

In *And Then There Were None*, Christie asks us whether the people trapped on the island are even human by referencing them as animals in a zoo. This is my own opinion, but I believe that the answer she intends for us to take from her book is that, yes (unfortunately), these people are very human. Perhaps she is even suggesting that the capacity for such evil is part of what it means to be human. A modern writer need not ship a bunch of fictional evildoers off to an island and start taking potshots at them to explore these questions.

There are many, many ways to write a book that questions what it means to be human. I don't assign *And Then There Were None* to my students so that they can answer the question exactly as Christie did. I assign it so that they can consider the question at the heart of it and then go write their own answers. In answer to the question driving this essay, one way I acknowledge Christie's influence in my own books, while still stepping out of her shadow, is to strip away all the detail of one of her stories and ask myself, "What's left?" In the case of *And Then There Were None*, the thing that's left is the mystery of what hides at the core of a human heart. Is it evil or is it goodness or can it be both? I could spend my whole career exploring that conundrum without ever treading on Dame Agatha's toes.

By the same token, I don't assign *Murder on the Orient Express* to inspire my students to write convoluted ensemble pieces wherein every single suspect is guilty of the murder of a truly despicable person. I assign it so that they can think deeply about the damage that the truly despicable person did when he murdered a child and caused the deaths of three other people. This is the kind of sin that ripples outward, devastating everyone who loved those people. In *Murder on the Orient Express*, Christie assembles twelve such devastated people and allows them to murder the man who scarred their lives irrevocably and escaped the law's punishment—a result that is, honestly, pretty satisfying. But is it right?

Is it just that Hercule Poirot, who devotes decades of his life to pursuing justice, allows these premeditated murderers to go free? The blurry boundaries between what is right, what is legal, what is just, and what is moral are fascinating to me. Exploring those boundaries will undergird my entire career as both a writer and a scholar. As a teacher, I find that few things are more fun than to assemble a group of students who have read *Murder on the Orient Express* and ask, "So did Poirot do the right thing? Are you okay with the premeditated murder of a defenseless man? Does it make the murder okay if we presume that the defenseless man remained such a danger to others, including children, that he probably needed killing?"

When I write an unreliable narrator, it helps me to know that *The Murder of Roger Ackroyd* exists, not because I want to copy it, but because I don't. When I write a naïve narrator, it helps me to know about Poirot's dear friend Captain Hastings, just as it helps me to be familiar with Sherlock Holmes' friend John Watson. And when I write a character who is much, much more than they seem, it helps me to remember the foolhardiness of anyone who ever underestimated Miss Jane Marple, the patron saint of women who know that they remain of value, even as they age.

Recently, I was reminded of the long shadow of the Dame when my novel *The Traitor Beside Her* received what is surely the most prominent coverage of my career, a review in the *Washington Post*. The reviewer said nice things about its "cinematic plot" and its "vividly drawn" characters. Even better, from the point of view of an admirer of Agatha Christie's art and craft, the *Washington Post* mentioned my Christie scholarship and, in the same sentence, called my novel a "Christie-inspired closed room mystery."

Did I consciously evoke Christie's work while writing this book? No, I didn't. It's an espionage novel set during World War II. If I had any fictional character in the back of my mind, it was probably James Bond, albeit a young and inexperienced female James Bond in high heels and lipstick. Nevertheless, Dame Agatha did get there first, as anyone who has read the woman-led World War II espionage novel *N or M?* will know, but this doesn't mean that my story of a young woman tasked with breaking codes and unmasking spies isn't wholly my own.

Did it bother me to see my work described as inspired by someone else's?

Dear Reader, what do you think?

(The answer is a resounding no. I've never been more honored.)

Fair Play in Cozies

J.A. Hennrikus

The mystery writer balances keeping the reader informed while hiding the truth from them. We're tricksters, but we need to maintain a balance of trust with our audience. Our aim is to mystify, not frustrate. Playing fair is an unwritten rule, a balancing act that must be followed. That said, what does it mean in this new century, a century after the Golden Age of the puzzle mystery, an antecedent of the cozy? This essay will explore the role of fair play in the cozy.

But first, exploring this relationship between author and reader is worth considering since it helps define fair play. The significance of mystification is explored by John G. Cawelti in *Adventure, Mystery and Romance*:

> A successful detective story of this sort must not only be solved, it must mystify, and to effectively serve the basic psychological functions of the classic formula, it must mystify in particular ways: we must truly be able to suspect a person whom we do not wish to be proved guilty before, finally, the crime is brought home to some person with whom our identification is minimal. These two interests—ratiocination and mystification—stand in a tense and difficult relationship to each other. If either one is overstressed, the story will be less effective. Thus, the first artistic problem of the classical detective writer is to establish the proper balance between reasoning and mystification.[1]

The history of fair play begins with the puzzle mystery, a staple of the "Golden Age of Mysteries" which took place between World War I and World War II. The authors, and readers, of the time took fair play very seriously. The reader had to have all the clues available to them in the novel; the writer needed to do whatever they could to misdirect the reader. There were several articles written about the "rules" of the genre. Definitions of these rules vary. S.S. Van Dine, pseudonym of Willard Huntington Wright, defined twenty rules. His preface said that

> the Detective story is a kind of intellectual game. It is more—it is a sporting event. And for the writing of detective stories there are very definite laws—unwritten,

perhaps, but none the less binding; and every respectable and self-respecting con-cocter of literary mysteries lives up to them. Herewith, then, is a sort of Credo, based partly on the practice of all the great writers of detective stories, and partly on the promptings of the honest author's inner conscience. To wit:

- The reader must have equal opportunity with the detective for solving the mystery. All clues must be plainly stated and described.
- No willful tricks or deceptions may be placed on the reader other than those played legitimately by the criminal on the detective himself.[2]

While these two rules make a certain kind of sense, some of Van Dine's other rules include no love interests, that the detective must be a detective, that there has to be a corpse, that the death can never be an acci-dent or a suicide, and that the motive has to be personal. While Van Dine's rules are worth reading, they limit the twenty-first-century mystery writer in too many ways. Particularly the cozy writer, who often uses the love affair trope and entirely depends on amateur detectives.

Ronald A. Knox defined ten rules in his "A Detective Story Deca-logue." They include only allowing one secret passage, that the murder weapon shouldn't require a long scientific explanation, that the detective must not commit the crime, that no supernatural solutions are allowed, and that "the stupid friend of the detective, the Watson, must not conceal from the reader any thoughts which pass through his mind; his intelli-gence must be slightly, but very slightly, below that of the average read-er."[3] An entire essay could be written about these two sets of rules and the problematic biases of some of them, but that is not the goal of this essay.

In 1928 Anthony Berkeley formalized meetings of fellow puzzle mys-tery writers and founded the Detection Club. Members of the Detection Club were sworn to an oath, promising to follow the specific rules of the puzzle mystery genre. For the purposes of this article, let's consider the four rules of detective fiction outlined in the oath of the Detection Club, presumed to have been written by Dorothy Sayers. In her article "Myster-ies: Rules of the Genre," Kay House lists Sayers' rules:

1. The detective must solve the case only using his or her wits.
2. No vital clue can be withheld from the reader.
3. Gangs, super-criminals, trap doors, hidden rooms and other contrivances should be used sparingly.
4. Poisons unknown to science are forbidden.[4]

House also states two other rules of the genre not stated in the oath but central to the puzzle mystery. First, the puzzle must be central to the plot. Second, justice must prevail in the end.

Today the cozy mystery has its roots in the traditional puzzle mystery. What role does fair play have for today's cozy author? Do cozy readers still expect rules of fair play be followed?

Here are my suggestions for the "rules" of fair play for the modern cozy. The cozy mystery, as previously stated, is a relation to the puzzle mystery, but not necessarily a direct descendant. There are adaptations to the old rules that must be made to support the modern cozy.

The authors create a world that has heightened reality, and they create rules around that world. The authors need to follow their own rules.

We all know that in real life the chance of a writer, master gardener, night market owner, baker, crafter, clambake owner or shopkeeper solving murders regularly is non-existent. Yet amateur sleuths play an important role, a central role in cozy mysteries. Getting involved in the crime needs to make sense *in the world of the book*. This can be tenuous, but the reader needs to make the leap without losing faith in the author.

The sleuth needs to be able to put together clues in a way that law enforcement or other detectives cannot and do it in a believable way.

The conceit of the cozy is that the amateur sleuth has access to information that other people in roles of authority do not. In other words, fair play means that the amateur sleuth does not have access to a spectrometer, but they do understand what sort of fertilizer is used in a garden, or the drug history of a neighbor, or how someone usually takes their coffee.

While their wits are important, cozy sleuths use other means to solve the mystery. They may have information and facts from connections to authority. Or they may avail themselves to unexpected technology or inside knowledge. The sleuth is the only person who puts the facts and information together in the correct way, but it's more of a community effort in today's cozy. The sleuth must solve the case through their investigations using whatever means at their disposal. Again, their investigations and techniques need to make sense in the world the author has created.

No vital clue can be withheld from the reader.

This rule stands. Though today's cozies are not always puzzle mysteries, they are still mysteries. The reader and author are playing a game of misdirection. The writer may hide a clue, or work hard to confuse the reader, but no vital clue should be withheld.

Justice must prevail in the end.

While justice doesn't play a part in fair play, it does play a role in reader satisfaction. Part of the reader/author promise is that the world will be made right again. Justice can and does come in many different forms, though usually it results in an arrest and the perpetrator of the crime being removed from the community.

The puzzle/mystery must be central to the plot.

The mystery of the cozy is central to the plot. There are subplots and story arcs that go from book to book in a series. And some of the plots may be less about the mystery and more about how the mystery affects a relationship, situation or part of the community that is central to the series. In cozy mysteries, the community is disrupted. The goal of the book is to heal that disruption. The how of the healing is the mystery.

Gangs, super-criminals, trap doors, hidden rooms and other contrivances should be used sparingly.

Readers would be as frustrated by a contrived solution to a mystery today as they were a century ago. At the same time, playing with hidden rooms and master criminals can work in a well-constructed plot. For fair play purposes, they need to make sense and be supported by the rest of the story. The original rule, that they be used sparingly, stands.

Causes of death need to be plausible but not necessarily possible.

While the original rules explicitly stated that "poisons unknown to science are forbidden," in today's cozy science itself has manufactured more ways to combine and change the chemistry of many items that will react in unknown ways. What seemed impossible a hundred years ago is more than possible today. That said, made-up poisons do need to be based in possibility, so some research is required—another reason cozy authors' browser history is a tangled web.

Cozies use a variety of methods of death, oftentimes tied into the theme of the book. Some cozies are more realistic than others, and the manners of death in those books will need to be more convincing. What's important is that the crime is plausible in the world of the book, not that it's necessarily possible in the real world. Fair play means that the author has to create a crime that makes sense and then provide clues to the reader. Adding a layer of science that only the author knows, and never hints at, isn't fair play.

The solution can't come out of the blue.

Though fair play in cozies may not be as rigid as for puzzle mysteries, the solution still needs to make sense based on the information the author has given the reader. Again, the author's job is to hide the clues but not to withhold them. Bringing in a heretofore unknown relative, not letting the reader in on a crucial conversation, depending on obscure knowledge—none of that is fair play.

One of the joys of reading, and writing, cozies is that we enter a realm where wrongs are righted, justice prevails, community comes together, and the world is a kinder, gentler place. As writers, we engage with our readers in a clash of wits. We have to balance surprise and obfuscation with fair play, to entertain rather than frustrate. Though the rules of fair play are different than they were a century ago, the goal is the same: to keep the reader coming back for more.

NOTES

1. John G. Cawelti, *Adventure, Mystery and Romance: Formula Stories as Art and Popular Fiction* (Chicago: University of Chicago Press, 1976) 107.

2. Willard Huntington Wright, "Twenty Rules for Writing Detective Stories by S.S. Van Dine." Wired, "Beyond the Beyond," 10 January 2019. https://www.wired.com/beyond-the-beyond/2019/01/s-s-van-dines-twenty-rules-writing-detective-stories/.

3. Ronald A. Knox, "A Detective Story Decalogue," *Detective Fiction: A Collection of Critical Essays*, ed. Robin W. Winks (Englewood Cliffs, NJ: Prentice-Hall, 1980) 200–202.

4. Kay House, "Mystery: Rules of the Genre," *Holly Lisle's Vision* #9, April–May 2002, 14 Oct. 2007. http://www.cs.appstate.edu/~sjg/detectionclub/detections02.pdf.

The Accessibility of Cozies

How Playing Fair Is How Cozies Endure

ANDREA J. JOHNSON

Cozies have become popular today because they include an amateur sleuth whose profession aids in the solution of the crime, thereby giving the audience a level of plot "accessibility" not available with a technique-driven detective at the helm—such as Arthur Conan Doyle's Sherlock Holmes or Agatha Christie's Hercule Poirot. This open communication between author, reader, and gumshoe gives the cozy audience an opportunity to solve the caper alongside the investigator. Modern cozies like my novel, *Poetic Justice*, adhere to the classic mystery structure of the Golden Age while expanding upon the genre by integrating aspects of the sleuth's career, personality, and point of view into the overall detection and resolution of the crime.

First, let us briefly outline the elements of a cozy mystery. Most cozies are set in a small town, but this is not a requirement as long as the setting is somewhat secluded or sets a tone of community and shared values. *Poetic Justice* mainly takes place in the courtroom of a rural township, but a national baking contest, a Hollywood movie set, or a dinner party will do if a suitable microcosm is not available. When everyone has a communal connection, the sleuthing becomes easier for the amateur detective, and the suspect list remains visible to the audience at all times. Thus, the gumshoe (often female) relies on her friends, family, and enemies to inform her crime solving. She may also have a relationship with the victim, good or bad, that motivates her to take the case and informs her modes of detection. For example, my protagonist, Victoria, must solve the murder of a judge when the drug trial of her high school nemesis goes sour. In other detective fiction subgenres—hard-boiled, police procedurals, spy thrillers—the reader or investigator may know the identity of the killer upfront, so the focus becomes *can they catch the culprit before it is too late?* In a cozy, the sleuth may interact with the killer but the murderer's identity does not surface until the end. Humor also plays a vital role by acting as a counterbalance to the mayhem although most cozies avoid depicting serious bloodshed. It helps that the killers in these stories aren't sociopaths or ne'er-do-wells. Instead, they are rational and articulate. During the story, they hide in plain sight and interact with the protagonist in a relatively normal manner, although this camaraderie with the investigator inevitably leads to them explaining their motives upon capture—usually personal motives that connect with the community's milieu.

But for a cozy to be truly satisfying, the plot must adhere to the rules of fair play. According to Martin Edwards' *The Golden Age of Murder*, these rules first came to fruition in 1928 when British mystery writer Ronald Knox introduced the *Best Detective Stories of the Year* anthology with what he called a "Decalogue" or the Ten Commandments for detective fiction (118). Later adopted by the Detection Club—a group of British mystery writers that included such greats as Agatha Christie and Dorothy L. Sayers—these rules aided the audience's ability to play along with the sleuth and shaped a growing genre. Some of these rules included: "The criminal must be someone mentioned in the early part of the story…. No accident must ever help the detective…. The detective must not himself commit the crime…. The detective must not light on any clues that are not instantly produced for the inspection of the reader" (118). Fair play lets the audience become an active participant in the story. With all of those moving parts in the structure of a cozy, fans of the genre not only benefit from the emotional highs and lows of the plot but also the thrill of victory and the agony of defeat that comes with getting the puzzle right or wrong. The level of engagement possible in these stories mimics the passions, tension, and suspense of our daily lives.

Poetic Justice follows the typical cozy format and the rules of fair play— female protagonist, small town, explicit clues—but the profession for my sleuth, Victoria, is a courtroom stenographer. This is an occupation that I haven't seen used in cozies before and one that has the potential to provide readers new insight into the drama of the courtroom from a perspective that's different from the judge or attorneys. This career-based theme also helps to expand upon Knox's fair play rules because it gives the audience a context in which to piece together their puzzle. They know that Victoria will only be able to view and analyze the clues based on her acute skills of observation, organization, concentration, and attentiveness as a court reporter. As a result, she is often able to come to conclusions that elude the police:

> "Stevenson didn't write that letter." I clasped my hands, determined to make him believe. "Or if he wrote it, he wrote it under duress. The signature on that letter read Spencer O. Stevenson. I've seen his signature before. I am 100

percent sure his middle initial is 'J' for James. I should have known as many times as I've looked up his full name to put on the coversheet of trial transcripts. Whoever wrote that letter didn't know his middle name—" [Johnson 197].

Of course, cozies require a certain suspension of disbelief with regard to how much the amateur detective's profession or skill can assist with crime detection. However, this discrepancy plays into the audience's unspoken desire that the ordinary person can rise to the challenge of an extraordinary situation and thus opens the door for the reader to solve the crime alongside the sleuth.

George N. Dove, author of *The Reader and the Detective Story*, puts these ideas into perspective by highlighting how the modern detection story uses the relationship between the author and the reader to build and relieve tension. "If the detective story is a game ... there must be definitional rules that do not simply regulate the playing of the game but make it possible for the game to be played" (19). By melding the rules of fair play with the professional skills of the protagonist, the audience feels a sense of surety that a solution is nigh even if they have not been able to follow each one of the author's clues and red herrings. This surety leads to a calming effect that permits the audience to turn a portion of their concern to the characters' plight rather than worry over the complexities of the mystery plot. Granted, the reader should still be pleased when the murderer's identity unfolds. The author wants the audience to exclaim, *I suspected as much!* or gasp, *I didn't expect that, but it makes perfect sense in retrospect!* To surprise without breaking the rules of fair play is to achieve mastery within the genre.

Cozy authors achieve this mastery by giving their protagonists a moral compass that is stronger than the average. Justice must prevail. Unlike hard-boiled detective tales or thrillers, cozy endings leave no room for ethical ambiguity. Ross Macdonald's essay "The Writer as Detective Hero" takes this idea a step further by theorizing that traditional mystery writers tend to create sleuths that are a reflection of their personal values whether conscious of this or not. "A close paternal or fraternal relationship between writer and detective is a marked peculiarity of the form. Throughout its history, from Poe to Chandler and beyond, the detective hero has represented his creator and carried his values into action in society" (295–296). While the gumshoe in *Poetic Justice* isn't a mirror reflection of the author, the character Victoria Justice does embody the author's view of her profession—and hence, one of the themes of the novel—whereupon the courtroom stenographer becomes that last bastion for morality. She upholds the profession's tenets of hyper-conscious accuracy, honesty, and neutrality in the face of the law. In Victoria's first-person telling of the tale, she explains how these elements might not compute with Joe Q. Public but consistently save the day in the courtroom … as well as in the delicate matter of her judge's murder.

Cozies further capitalize on the fair play rules and the classic mystery structure by ramping up characterization. The players in each story must pop off the page in a manner that will make readers care about their personality and storylines long after the novel ends. That's one of the reason why the sleuths in cozies are amateurs. The protagonist becomes a part of the investigation because they work with, care for, or share DNA with the parties involved in the crime, which feeds into the motivation of the players. On the other hand, a professional gumshoe's detachment from the overall scenario places the spotlight more on the procedure of detection. But do not mistake a detective's amateur status as a writer's attempt to dilute the plot; view it as the author's attempt to personalize the protagonist. By developing stories that make fewer demands on the sleuth's methods of detection, authors can build a characterization that includes life lessons like love and loss. This humanizing aspect appeals to cozy fans who might not remember one plot from another, but they'll recall the overall theme. The challenge for Victoria throughout *Poetic Justice* is learning to stand up for herself, and this lesson becomes apparent in every relationship, most notably when she befriends a disgraced local cop to aid in her detection. In most cozies, she'd fall head over heels in love with him, but since she can't fully trust him, she never allows herself to become the clichéd damsel in distress. Her guarded approach saves her from duplicity while solving the murder but also provides a notable moral dilemma readers can debate as Victoria's life continues in future novels.

Another way cozies seek to expand upon traditional mysteries and the fair play rules is point of view. Viewpoint plays a crucial role in determining the overall effectiveness of character development by providing the perspective through which the audience observes and experiences the events of the story. Because today's cozies generally use first- or a tight third-person viewpoint, cozy audiences never need to decipher what the investigator is thinking through the filter of secondary character or narrator because cozies utilize the gumshoe's perspective. But it was not always that way. Detective fiction as we know it began with Edgar Allan Poe's short story "The Murders in the Rue Morgue" published in *Graham's Magazine* in 1841. According to Robert Lowndes' essay "The Contributions of Edgar Allan Poe," Poe's story invents the basic plot repeated throughout detective fiction—the sleuth's associate narrates their collective adventure, and the pair use research, interviews, and reasoning rather than brute force or physical violence to solve the crime. This reliance on intellectual tools resonates throughout the story but is somewhat tainted by the fact that the use of a narrator distances the audience from the detective's true process.

However, according to Patricia Craig and Mary Cadogan, authors of *The Lady Investigates*, Anna Katharine Green's *The Leavenworth Case* (1878) is the literary work that brings the detective mystery to the forefront in America and solidifies this removed point of view (11). Green's story is set in New York City and revolves around the murder of a prosperous merchant in the library of his mansion. The book introduces a detective, Ebenezer Gryce, although the tale unfolds from the point of view of Raymond, a lawyer who represents the deceased. Readers may recognize this sidekick point of view as a staple of Sherlock Holmes and many of Agatha Christie's Poirot novels. Since the lawyer in *The Leavenworth Case* is an outsider looking in, we can only see a small portion of the crime from his skewed perspective. With each new clue, his knowledge grows, but we do not get the full picture from the mouth of the expert investigator until the end. For the most part, this first-person technique of having the supporting character lead and shape the narrative succeeds, but the technique presents a major problem if the audience gets ahead of the narrator. A narrator who is slow or bumbling may cause the audience to lose interest. The author also runs the risk of creating a point of view character who becomes a mere conduit for exposition or a narrator whose sole purpose is to ask naive questions of the superior sleuth. Both of these problems are tedious and make the audience aware of the filter through which the story unfolds.

To avoid this problem, *Poetic Justice* begins at a moment when Victoria is vulnerable and on the brink of change. She speaks directly to the audience about the transformation she undergoes during her story, and this connection helps ingratiate Victoria to the reader: "I hadn't seen Langley Dean in ten years. When we last spoke, she'd pushed me into the school pool while I was wearing Bickerton High's Scrappy the Seabird mascot uniform. The useless velvet wings and doughy web-footed moon boots wilted under the weight of the water and dragged me below the surface faster than a battleship anchor" (Johnson 1). The first-person viewpoint aids in establishing that this is a character-driven story and gives the reader an intimate perspective into the psychological journey Victoria undergoes during her struggle to understand the new world emerging around her. She overcomes vulnerability through the realization that she needs to take charge of her life if she wants to change the future and rewrite the past—a concept that is relatable to the readers and allows them to place themselves in Victoria's world if they so desire. With the first-person viewpoint, the audience only knows what Victoria knows. While this is limiting, because Victoria can only describe events she experiences firsthand or secondhand through character interaction, this inability to see from multiple angles aids in maintaining the book's mystery elements. The audience doesn't know what's coming next and neither does our protagonist. So while Victoria's hunches about her nemesis prove correct, Langley Dean's true motives to help rather than hurt go unnoticed until the end due to the reader's narrow viewpoint.

While this unpredictability keeps cozies fresh, these traditional mysteries ultimately work because of a specific format that includes a complex puzzle, an amateur sleuth, and a logical conclusion supported by the rules of fair play. All of these elements are significant because they encourage the audience to solve the crime in tandem with the detective while enjoying the escapism of a cozy community that mirrors their own. While some may see this humanizing shift to career, personality, and viewpoint as a dilution of the genre, modern cozies like *Poetic Justice* use these changes to build a more complex narrative and subvert the idea that a heroine must wait for the hero to take control. She can be her own hero—and, by extension, the reader can become his own hero. Cozies highlight that the average person has the ability to rise to the challenge of extraordinary circumstances, a valuable lesson in our self-made society and one that keeps bringing cozy readers back to the page.

From Rue Morgue to the Craft Cozy

The Evolution of the Traditional Mystery

Peggy Ehrhart

My journey from mystery reader to mystery writer was a long one. I discovered the genre in graduate school, when an evening curled up with a whodunit provided a welcome break after a day in the company of Beowulf or John Milton. A few decades writing for scholarly publications honed my writing skills but also made me yearn for a more creative outlet. When I decided to write fiction, it seemed only natural that I should attempt a mystery—a mystery in the traditional style that I had enjoyed so much as a reader.

The traditional mystery is a narrative form invented by Edgar Allan Poe in "The Murders in the Rue Morgue." It was developed by Arthur Conan Doyle in his Sherlock Holmes stories and brought to its peak in England before and after World War I, with writers like G.K. Chesterton, Agatha Christie, Dorothy Sayers, and Josephine Tey.

The basics of the traditional mystery are simple. We must have a sleuth, a victim, and a killer—it's almost essential that the crime in question be a murder, rather than something less serious. The stakes must be high and the motives must be dire. But beyond sleuth, victim, and killer, we must have a challenging puzzle—because, rather than dwelling on violence and gore, the traditional mystery emphasizes the sleuth's intellect and the process by which the sleuth arrives at the identity of the killer. Poe called this process "ratiocination," from *ratio*, the Latin word for "reason." The traditional mystery is profoundly comforting—and humanistic, one might say—because it depicts a world in which good always triumphs over evil and human reason is the means by which that triumph is achieved. It's no coincidence that G.K. Chesterton, a noted Catholic thinker, made his sleuth, Father Brown, a Catholic priest.

In order for the sleuth to be puzzled long enough to make for an entertaining plot, more than one person has to be suspected of the murder.

The sleuth proceeds by identifying all possible suspects and then ruling them out one by one until only the actual killer remains.

This is where clues come in. A clue can be an object, a word, a sound, a sight. It can even be an absence, as in Conan Doyle's "Silver Blaze," where the fact that a dog *doesn't* bark is significant. A clue is anything that provides, or seems to provide, information leading to the killer's identity. Most of the clues in a traditional mystery are, however, false clues or "red herrings." Red herrings seem to implicate a particular suspect, but then that suspect proves not to be the killer. The traditional mystery requires plenty of suspects since the main story-telling consists of the sleuth following up on clues, so in a skillfully plotted mystery, the red herrings should be many and they should be obvious.

The term "red herring" purportedly comes from the world of hunting. As a dog is learning to follow a scent while tracking game, it is tested by dragging an odiferous smoked fish across the trail. The dog must learn to resist this interesting distraction and remain focused on the scent that leads to the true quarry—just as the successful sleuth must recognize the real clues that actually lead to the killer.

These real clues, however, should not be obvious. If they were, the reader would solve the murder before the sleuth did and the whole fun of the mystery would be lost. People don't normally relish the experience of being fooled, but fans of the mystery genre actively seek it out, because the climactic revelation of the truth when the sleuth's work is complete provides such gratifying relief. Only the sleuth recognizes the real clues—or actually doesn't even recognize them as *clues* but as an observant person notices things and remembers them. It's useful to think of the real clues as random puzzle pieces. Eventually the sleuth recognizes *something* as the missing piece that, with other random pieces, forms a coherent whole. That's when the light bulb goes on in the sleuth's mind. There's an a-ha moment, and the murder is solved.

The world that the sleuth inhabits is crucial to the form. It must offer a ready supply of victims, killers, and clues. Robinson Crusoe on a desert island would not serve! My first mystery series—all two books of it—was the Maxx Maxwell mysteries, *Sweet Man Is Gone* and *Got No Friend Anyhow*, long out of print but available in e-book form. Both titles are based on classic blues tunes and my sleuth, Maxx (Elizabeth) Maxwell, is a blues singer and bandleader. Her band, Maxximum Blues, is a struggling New York City bar band, and Maxx herself lives in a downbeat apartment building in Hackensack, New Jersey. The Maxx Maxwell mysteries are traditional mysteries in structure and, though the settings are gritty rehearsal studios and grungy bars, and many of the characters dwell on the edges of society, the puzzle aspect of the mystery is uppermost and violence and vulgarity are minimal.

Maxx's world consists of her bandmates: Jimmy, the guitar player (victim in *Sweet Man Is Gone*, eventually replaced by Stan on guitar); Michael, the bass player; Neil, the keyboard player; and Dom, the drummer. Maxx also spends time with her neighbor, Leon, an intellectual African American law student who reads Shakespeare for fun. The band members come together for gigs and for weekly rehearsals. Their varied personalities make for conflict, both with each other and with Maxx, who struggles to keep her band together, and the ensemble offers possible suspects and clues—notably, in this case, Stan, as will be discussed below.

Maxx's world offers many crime-solving opportunities. In *Sweet Man Is Gone*, Jimmy is found dead on the pavement outside the apartment building where he lived on a high floor. He has seemingly jumped, and his death is ruled a suicide. But Maxx can't believe that Jimmy, the dashing and talented guitar player she held responsible for her band's success, and who she also had a crush on, would kill himself, and she resolves to figure out what really happened. Note that this ploy—amateur sleuth must step in because the police don't think the dead person was murdered—is a tried and true one in mystery fiction.

Maxx's world, and the band itself, offer many possible suspects, with clues—or are they red herrings?—pointing to them. Stan is annoying with his constant guitar noodling and lack of social graces, and Maxx fired him and recruited Jimmy in his place. Thus, he's a prime suspect in Jimmy's murder, with his motive being a desire to get his old spot back (which he eventually does). Bart, connected with the studio where Maxx's band rehearses, is another suspect—because Jimmy supposedly knew that a charity concert Bart had advertised was a scam. Then there is Monique, a woman still pining for Jimmy after a breakup, and the jazz guitarist who is in love with Monique. Did he want Jimmy out of the way so he could win Monique back? And Maxx learns that Jimmy grew up in Nashville, son of a country and western duo. Has family dysfunction caused by his father's philandering somehow followed him to New York City?

In *Got No Friend Anyhow*, Maxx's new love interest, Rick, who is also producing her group's first CD, disappears and is later found dead. Knowing Rick as she did, Maxx recognizes a clue to his death in a photo linking him to a band he was part of long ago, and she believes that this clue is a better lead to his killer than leads the police may be pursuing. Another clue, a letter from a former girlfriend still aggrieved about losing him, takes Maxx to a gig in a Village club where the former girlfriend is performing and where Maxx catches sight of a young woman who might be Rick's daughter. Complication leads to complication, and suspects multiply.

I also wrote a few short stories set in Maxx Maxwell's world, some featuring her and some not, but all exploiting the possibilities for suspects and clues to be found in a blues band environment. Left-handed guitar players can often be identified as lefties by the way they hold a guitar. Acoustic guitar players often cultivate long fingernails on the hand they pick with to serve as built-in picks. And I had fun with this clue: a slide guitar player makes his own bottleneck slides by cutting the necks off glass bottles. Maxx locates him when she comes upon a trash bag containing bottles with missing necks.

When I embarked on the Knit & Nibble series, it wasn't because Maxx Maxwell's world lacked victims, killers, and suspects—or entertaining clues. It was because I realized that most fans of the traditional mystery would rather spend their time in a cozy kitchen with a tea kettle whistling on the stove than in a dive bar smelling of stale beer and decades-old cigarette smoke. So I became a cozy mystery writer.

Since the cozy mystery is a subcategory of the traditional mystery, everything I've said so far about the structure of the traditional mystery applies to the cozy mystery as well, but cozies have their own distinctive character.

Originally the word "cozy" was applied dismissively. Mysteries that focused on domestic life and featured tea pots and cats couldn't be taken seriously or put in the same class as those written by the Golden Age masters. But readers ultimately triumphed. Nothing succeeds like success. Readers bought and read cozies, so publishers published more and more cozies and here we are. And it doesn't hurt that cozy mysteries offer a contrast to the real world, which is becoming less cozy by the minute.

Traditional mysteries frequently had amateur sleuths, even female sleuths: think Miss Marple. Cozy mysteries almost always have amateur sleuths, and those sleuths are almost always female. If the traditional mystery was often set in a charming small town, the cozy mystery is almost always set in a charming small town. For one thing, a female amateur sleuth can operate easily in a small town. Everyone knows everyone's business anyway and neighbors are happy to gossip. If the traditional mystery eschewed violence and gore, the cozy mystery often goes so far as to make the murder that kicks off the plot blatantly unrealistic. No one could seriously fear being garroted by a circular knitting needle, yet that is the murder weapon in my *Knitty Gritty Murder*. People are not often killed with poison anymore in real life, but it's a popular murder technique in cozies—and it can be administered in a cup of tea, which amusingly ties in with the cozy mystique. Moreover, it doesn't involve violence and it doesn't result in blood.

Readers come to cozy mysteries as much to escape into the cozy world they offer as to relish the spectacle of a sleuth solving a puzzle. In fact, I like to think of cozies as Martha Stewart with murders, and I believe that a chief pleasure of the cozy, sought out by dedicated cozy readers, is the Martha Stewart dimension. Cozies, one might say, are aspirational in the same way that the upscale lifestyle magazines are. The characters live in pretty houses decorated with pretty furniture and surrounded by pretty landscaping. They bake goodies, eat yummy meals, and give parties. The image of a corpse lying at the base of a picturesque stone wall covered with climbing roses has probably been imprinted on my mind as a result of streaming too many British mysteries—as has the image of police detectives following up a lead as they sip tea and nibble on scones in a charming cottage. But to me these images from British mysteries helped shape the cozy mystique, even if the series in which they figured were not explicitly cozy.

It is probably this Martha Stewart dimension of the cozy that has given rise to the mystery sub-subgenre known as the "craft cozy," though the term is something of a misnomer. Some cozies designated as craft cozies feature sleuths who are genuinely crafters, like my Knit & Nibble series, in which my sleuth Pamela Paterson is a devoted knitter and the founder of a knitting club. Others, however, might feature sleuths who are shop owners—purveyors of cheese, lingerie, antiques, candles, soap, scrapbooking supplies, or cookbooks, or sleuths who manage restaurants, own event-planning businesses, or organize clubs that involve crafts: scrapbooking, crochet, knitting. Because of cozies' link with crafts and food, they often include "bonus features" such as recipes or instructions for craft projects, so the reader can replicate the actual meals served or projects crafted in her favorite cozies.

The "crafts" in craft cozies also give the mysteries a "hook," a gimmick. The sleuth has an identity, a job, an avocation that sets the mystery in a certain world and gives the sleuth special talents, skills, or insight. Hooks are not peculiar to craft cozies—the hook in my Maxx Maxwell mysteries is that she is a musician, and one might say that the hook in the Father Brown mysteries is that he is a priest. But they are essential in craft cozies. A hook makes it more plausible that an amateur sleuth might finger a killer overlooked by the police, because someone with a specialized knowledge of, say, beekeeping might recognize a clue that the police are blind to.

In my Knit & Nibble mysteries, my sleuth is Pamela Paterson, a knitter and the founder of a knitting club in charming Arborville, New Jersey. She is also associate editor of *Fiber Craft* magazine and thus reads and edits articles dealing with all aspects of crafts that involve fiber. In the same way that Maxx's band members form an ensemble in the Maxx Maxwell mysteries, the members of the knitting club form an ensemble in the Knit & Nibble mysteries.

Besides Pamela, there are five regular members, though the reader becomes familiar with their spouses as well. The oldest member of the group is Nell Bascomb, in her eighties, an old-time liberal who thinks it wasteful to buy new clothes, walks everywhere she can, and doesn't approve of sugar. Her knitting projects consist of such charitable projects as knitted animals or Christmas stockings for the children at the local women's shelter. Holly Perkins and Karen Dowling are young women in their twenties. Holly is the more adventurous of the pair, both in her personal style and in her knitting projects, while Karen is Holly's opposite, shy and sweet, and devoted to her little daughter. Roland DeCamp, the only male member of the group, is a hard-driving corporate lawyer who took up knitting when his doctor suggested that it might lower his blood pressure. Bettina Fraser is Pamela's fellow sleuth, her best friend, and her across-the-street neighbor. She knits slowly, sometimes preferring to chat.

The club often entertains visiting members as well, and thus the ensemble absorbs characters who might be victims or suspects. The knitting club meetings offer Pamela a chance to observe these people closely and notice details that might later be significant.

How does Pamela's world give rise to murders that an amateur sleuth with expertise in knitting might feel compelled to solve? Here are some examples: A recruit to the Knit and Nibble club never shows up for her first meeting and is found dead in Pamela's shrubbery, stabbed with a knitting needle. Clues lie in a bin of yarn and knitting supplies given to Pamela by the victim's sister. The Knit and Nibble group has knit toy aardvarks to be sold at Arborville's town festival. Sales are to benefit the high school athletic program, whose mascot is an aardvark. The body of an unpopular teacher is found under the knitting club's booth with one of the aardvarks perched on his chest. Naturally the knitting club feels implicated and it seems only natural that Pamela and Bettina would apply themselves to the case. A major clue is a curious hand-knit hat they find in the dead man's house.

Other clues—or maybe red herrings—might be a noteworthy type of yarn or a knitting project that replicates the swath of knitting in which Mme. Defarge, from *A Tale of Two Cities*, recorded the names of those destined for the guillotine. A clue might be a knitting pattern linked in Celtic folklore to a love charm. A pair of socks worn by a suspect might bring to mind a pair the sleuth saw being knitted earlier. A knitted garment seen in a photo might later be recognized in person.

I don't want to give any of my plots away by explaining exactly how red herrings function to confuse the reader and how real clues come together in the mind of the sleuth, so I'm going to make up examples here. Red herrings that point to a suspect who is not actually the killer: The sleuth notices someone wearing a sweater identical to one the murder victim was wearing right before her death but which was missing from the crime scene. Probing further, the sleuth learns that the person wearing the sweater harbored a longstanding grudge against the murder victim. Moreover, the sweater-wearer refuses to say where she was at the time the murder took place.

These are red herrings, and they are eventually discounted: The victim had discarded the sweater in a help-yourself bin of used clothes and the suspect saw it and liked it and had no idea where it came from. People often bear grudges but don't act on the grudges. The suspect refuses to provide herself with an alibi because she was meeting a lover and wanted to keep the relationship secret.

And here are examples of real clues, well hidden, also invented: Suppose a key to untangling the mystery lies in recognizing a romantic relationship. The sleuth notices, without making a big deal of it, and in a scene where a great deal else is going on, that a man is wearing a sweater knit from yarn dyed a distinctive color. Later the sleuth chats with a woman who harvests natural plant materials to make her own dyes for her knitting projects and the woman displays a hank of wool dyed the same distinctive color as the sweater noticed earlier. Or a scarf in a noteworthy color is significant. Who made it? Who ended up with it? A visiting knitter's knitting bag tips over at a Knit and Nibble meeting and odds and ends of yarn spill out. The sleuth notes, without realizing the significance—*yet*—that a small ball of that same color of yarn is among the odds and ends. Later the sleuth encounters a woman bundled up in a winter outfit—an interesting outfit that deserves much description, but the flash of that noteworthy color at the neck is jumbled in with all the other description so the reader scarcely pays attention.

I would say then that almost any world can be the setting for a traditional mystery or its offshoot, the craft cozy. But if the sleuth is to be an amateur sleuth, the writer must make some attempt to explain why an amateur is jumping in rather than leaving the solution to the police. As I mentioned, one ploy is to have the death be ruled a suicide—but the sleuth knows the victim well enough to suspect that it wasn't. Or perhaps the sleuth thinks she could have prevented the murder but didn't and feels guilty. Or maybe the murder puts a group or institution the sleuth cares about in a bad light. The dead person might be a friend or a romantic interest, and the sleuth believes the police are not doing enough. Or maybe the sleuth believes the wrong person has been arrested and that person is a friend of the sleuth. Note that Poe used this in "The Murders in the Rue Morgue" as the justification for his amateur sleuth, Dupin, to get involved.

Most crucial, though, is that the sleuth is intimately familiar with the world in which the mystery unfolds. A gardener in New Jersey knows very well that crocus don't appear in September, that hosta are perennials but impatiens are annuals, and that butterflies are attracted to milkweed. Such specialized knowledge could easily unmask an imposter trying to fabricate an alibi. A bread-maker could recognize a rival baker's handiwork in the shape of a poisoned loaf. Or, to return to an example that might figure in my own Knit & Nibble series, a knitter might recognize the rarity of a particular yarn linked with a murder scene and use her contacts at the local yarn shop to track down the person who purchased it.

Thus, far from being a frivolous dilution of the serious traditional mystery, cozies—craft cozies in particular—represent a very logical development of the mystery genre. If the puzzle is the point and the sleuth is the puzzle solver, the worlds presented in craft cozies offer victims, sleuths, clues, and red herrings in abundance—enough puzzlement to satisfy the most discerning mystery fan.

Writing Multiple Series

Edith Maxwell

I write at least three books a year, and sometimes more, plus short stories. I was already writing two successful cozy mystery series in the spring of 2022 when my Kensington editor asked if I would write a new series set in California. I thought only briefly about my workload and responded with a resounding yes.

Crazy? Maybe, since I also have a new historical project not under contract that I'm passionate about. But the chance to create a series set in my home state was so exciting, I couldn't refuse.

I've been asked many times how I do it. Over the years I've developed a multi-faceted approach that works for me.

Several years ago, I consulted about their tips and tricks with a few prolific author friends who also write multiple series: Leslie Budewitz, Amanda Flower, Catriona McPherson, and the now-late Sheila Connolly. With their permission, I include some of their pointers here too.

Taking the Work Seriously

Primary in making my ambitious goals work for me is that writing mystery novels and short crime fiction is my full-time day job. I left my last place of employment in 2013, so I've been at this for a decade. I have nowhere else to go every morning except upstairs to my office in the house I share with my partner.

When I made my exit from my last software technical writing position, a number of friends asked how retirement was. My response never varied. "I'm not retired. This is just my next day job." And I treat the writing as such. I show up at my desk by six every morning but Sunday and am ready to work by seven.

Time Management

Part of taking it seriously is managing my time. I write a daily to-do list that sits next to my desk, and the first item is always "Write."

Scheduling

I spend all morning on creative work, whether it's batting out a sparse first draft or working through many revision passes. If I'm writing a first draft, I set myself a goal of 1500 words a day and often exceed it.

Amanda Flower writes way more books than I do. Here's what she said: "My advice would be to give yourself a daily goal to stay on top of your deadlines. I try to write 4,000 words every day. Sometimes I can do that in six hours, sometimes it takes 12! Just depends."

My appointment with my manuscript in the mornings is sacred time, especially that first hour. Hugh knows not to knock on my office door from seven to eight unless someone is bleeding or the house is on fire.

Sheila Connolly was also a morning writer. "I know I have a morning brain. I can get in several hours of writing/editing before lunch (after reading emails, etc.), but by mid-afternoon my brain just isn't working as well, so I do tasks that don't require creative thinking."

I take an exercise break at around eleven or twelve. It's usually a brisk hour's walk outdoors, during which I sometimes talk out loud to myself about the story's plot, and then I eat lunch. I reserve the afternoons for what I call the business of being an author: writing blog posts, arranging appearances, studying the craft, accounting, and all the other bits that don't involve creative energy. I also save the afternoons for things like haircuts and doctor visits.

My evenings are for eating, reading, and wasting time on social media. Each writer obviously will find her own creative time. The most important thing is to schedule it and honor it.

About twice a year, I take myself off to a retreat cottage alone for an intensive writing week, and then I work morning, afternoon, and night.

Focusing

I like to really focus when I'm writing a first draft. If I come to something I need to research, and it won't change the course of the story, I type "[CHECK THIS]." Going back to research those bits is my first revision pass. Because we all know that if you go onto the Internet to check one thing, you might not be back for three hours.

By preference I would charge straight through the first draft, writing every day until it's done. But publishers don't care about my preferences, and I might get copy edits back on a book in a different series or proofs to read in yet another series. Those demands are short-term—my editor needs them back within two or three weeks—and my book isn't due for three more months. So I pause the first draft, focus on the edits or proofs, and send them in. Then I can get back to the first draft.

Leslie Budewitz takes the same approach. "Tackle your edits, send them off, and celebrate your accomplishment. Then return to the WIP, which will have been waiting quietly in a comfy chair, confident that you will return and give it your full attention as soon as you can."

Tracking Due Dates

I also keep a hand-drawn four-year calendar on the wall above my laptop. The only things on it are due dates and release dates. I can tell at a glance when X book is due, when I need to start promotion for Y book's release, and how long I have left in a particular contract.

Leslie has a great approach. "When you write more than one series, you're always living in more than one world at a time. And while that can be a challenge, it's also a great joy. You know the worlds, you created them, you're (mostly) in control of them. You may be cogitating, planning, or writing a book in one series, while working with your publisher on the various stages of edits in another, promoting an earlier book or one in yet another series, and pitching a short story featuring yet more characters— or some combination of this creative chaos. Juggling it all can be confusing. My best advice? Be here now."

Promotion

Promoting any release takes a lot of time, hours that cut into valuable writing time. When one has two or three books coming out every year, it takes even more time and energy, especially when we're never sure which promotional activities connect the best with readers.

Catriona McPherson says, "Social media and publicity in general is hard. I always say it's not the writing of two or three books a year; it's having to pick one to be talking about. Maybe if all my stuff was with the same publisher (Ha!) we could thrash it out together, but as it stands, I'm always split."

Like Catriona, my releases aren't all from the same publisher, and sometimes I have a cluster of books coming out in one season and then none for the next half year. I just do my best, chipping away at those publicity bits in the afternoons.

Keeping Multiple Series Distinct

Another question I'm often asked is "Don't you mix up the characters in your various series?" I always respond that I don't. One of my role models in this business is (was, alas) my friend Sheila, who passed away in 2020 way too young. She wrote three and four books a year in different series. When I was starting out with more than one series, I asked her the same question. She said, "I don't confuse them. They're so real to me, how could I?"

Unique Settings

One important element is setting the stories in clearly demarcated locations. My Country Store Mysteries take place in a fictional southern Indiana town. The Cozy Capers Book Group Mysteries are set in a fictional tourist town on Cape Cod. The historical Quaker Midwife Mysteries take place in the town where I live in the northeast corner of Massachusetts— and in the late 1800s. And my new Cece Barton Mysteries feature the wine-producing Alexander Valley north of San Francisco. Each of these locations has its own weather, its own dialect, its own typical names.

Leslie agrees. "If you plan to write multiple series, choose carefully. Create [distinct] worlds you can fully inhabit to make moving between them easier and more enjoyable. And I guarantee that when you fully inhabit your story worlds, your readers will, too."

Unique Characters

Similarly, my protagonists have widely different occupations and family situations: a restaurant owner and chef with a regular crew and a cherished aunt nearby; a bike shop owner in her hometown and her book group cronies; a midwife in a mill town; and a wine bar manager who has moved to the town where her identical twin and young twin nephews live.

Each protagonist has her own quirks, her own food and exercise preferences, her own flaws. As with Sheila, they are all real to me.

Record-Keeping

I also keep detailed records about everything I know about people and places I make up, as well as real places and news events.

For example, my "Characters" file includes the police department: what color are the uniforms and the cruisers? Where is the police station located? And so on. The most information in the file is about my protagonist and the main recurring characters. What kind of handbag does she carry (if any)? Her eye color, her grandfather's name, any secrets in her past, what's in the trunk of her car in and in her refrigerator.

It's so important to begin recording these details at the start of a series and keep it current. I might not be aware of all these bits when I start writing, but as they reveal themselves, into the file they go, right up to book eleven. *Four Leaf Cleaver* is so far the highest-numbered book in any of my series, and I'm still adding to the file.

Amanda surprised me with this piece of advice for writers: "Take good notes on your own books with detailed character lists (I don't actually do this ... but I wish I did)."

Plotting

"But how do I keep plots distinct and fresh?" you might fairly ask.

One of the first things I do when I'm about to begin a new book is decide the method of murder and who dies by it. The plot follows from there. (I'm not an outliner except in the most minimal of ways. I basically follow my characters around and write down what they do.) I'm fond of killing people with poisons—fictionally!—but have never repeated a poison. My victims have also been stabbed, pushed, garroted, injected, but never (yet) shot with a gun. And I can safely say that I've never repeated a plot in 33 books.

With clearly delineated settings and casts of characters, even two similar plots come out completely different in the end.

Offloading

Another way I manage to produce this volume of work is by getting help and learning to say, "No."

I have a marvelous assistant who does my social media and promotional graphics. She's in Florida, I'm in Massachusetts, and we've never met in person. But I know my strengths, and graphics aren't among them. She is worth every penny I pay her.

My gorgeous website was created by a professional. She does the complicated stuff on it and runs regular maintenance so it stays safe from spamming and hacking. I can add my own book covers, short stories, photos, and events, but occasionally I'll hire her to do some of that work when I'm out of time.

I sometimes also barter. I have a talented friend around the corner who also knows graphics and owns Photoshop. Every year when I want to add new covers to the back of my bookmark, I send Margery the files to swap in and she sends back the print-ready version. In return, I offer her a choice of my new books.

I've also slid away from several volunteer opportunities after serving my term. There's only so much a woman can do while still maintaining a relationship, a family life, and a garden.

Staying Healthy

Writing multiple series can be stressful. I'd never be able to pull off this kind of work if I didn't stay healthy. I try to eat well, drink lots of water, and get regular exercise.

Amanda Flower agrees. "Exercise! I work out at least an hour every day. It keeps me sane."

Catriona says, "Healthy eating and exercise do indeed keep me sane! Then when I'm up against it, bacon and Buffy keep me sane."

Yeah. Dark chocolate and Goldfish crackers have gotten me through many a writing marathon.

I also find working at a standing desk keeps me healthy. I stand on a two-inch thick cushioned mat, which really helps my knees and feet. I find I move around so much more, often walking little laps in my office while I think, and I correct my posture and pull in my core as often as I remember.

Knowing when to stop is important, too. It's fine to knock off work, pour that cocktail, and watch a movie with your loved one. Taking a day of rest is good, too, which for me is usually Sunday, including an hour of unprogrammed worship with my fellow Quakers, followed by an afternoon couch nap, and usually phone chats with my sons. Catriona takes a full day off everything. "One day off a week—off work, off my phone, off social media—is my goal, quite often realised."

Find Your Own Path

It doesn't suit everyone to push themselves like authors of multiple series do. Some writers find the words arrive on the page more slowly. Many have family or work obligations—or both—that would make my kind of workload impossible. I have author pals who love combining their writing with other passions—art, music, travel—and consider the stress I'm under a nightmare.

For me, I'm living my dream, and I'm also earning a decent wage. Sure, I don't have clean closets or a perfectly organized basement. But you know what? I don't care.

PART TWO

Writing Theme

Crafts and the Cozy Mystery

SYBIL JOHNSON

I never thought I'd write mysteries. I loved reading them, but writing one seemed too hard—the plotting, the clues, the red herrings.... I was content to let others do the heavy lifting and enjoy the results.

Then, in my forties, I woke up one morning with the image in my head of a young woman finding the body of her painting teacher in her garden. Questions filled my mind. Who was this woman? What happened to her teacher? Could I write the story?

I decided to try.

I knew right away it would be a cozy because it's the type of mystery I most enjoy reading. I'd read many of them over the years, including ones that included crafts, and I thought I knew enough about them to write one.

I set the story in the world of decorative painting because I have a fair amount of experience with it. I first tried my hand at painting in the 1990s, when it was widely referred to as tole painting, and still enjoy it today.

There are scores of craft-based cozies featuring knitting, crocheting, pottery, glass blowing, scrapbooking.... The list goes on. But at the time I decided to try my hand at writing, none of them involved decorative painting. Sure, there were art-based mysteries, but they tended more toward the fine art end of the painting spectrum. I wanted to write stories that celebrated the craft I've enjoyed for so long.

With these decisions, my Aurora Anderson mystery series was born.

The main character in a cozy is an amateur sleuth who guides the investigation and is usually a woman, though that's not set in stone. The Candlemaking Mysteries by Tim Myers feature a man who inherits his great aunt's candle shop after she's murdered. And the sleuth in his Soap-making series is a man who helps run a family-owned business that sells all things soap related.

In my own case, my main character, Aurora Anderson, is a freelance computer programmer who enjoys painting in her spare time. I could have chosen to have her run a shop or business related to decorative painting. Plenty of cozies have characters who own or run stores. In the Needlecraft Mysteries by Monica Ferris, her main character inherits a needlecraft store when her sister is murdered. In the Seaside Knitter series by Sally Goldenbaum, the main character has a knitting shop where a group of women meet to knit, gossip and solve crimes.

Instead, I made Rory a programmer, partly because that's what I did for twenty years and partly because that profession gives her the freedom to make her own schedule. She can do her work at two in the morning if she needs to, giving her time to investigate in the middle of the day. Programmers also tend to be analytical, which is a good skill for an amateur sleuth.

I still wanted a store in the series, some place where painters could gather or where events could be held. I gave that job to Rory's mother, Arika, who owns Arika's Scrap 'n Paint, a decorative painting and scrapbook supply store in the fictional town of Vista Beach where my series is set. Rory spends a fair amount of time at the store helping out, so she has a chance to observe what goes on there. She's seen suspects questioned and even arrested at the store. She's attended events there that have yielded clues. At one of those, a character collapsed and later died.

Another feature of cozies is the setting. The crime usually takes place in a small, socially intimate community. That could be a small town, an isolated house or a group of people with a shared interest such as a craft. People gather together to paint, crochet, knit, etc. As they spend more time with each other, they get to know one another and become part of each other's lives.

People come and go in a crafting community. My experience is that new people are generally welcomed with open arms, but that doesn't have to be the case in a story. Newbies can upset the group dynamics, providing conflict and potential for crime. Even friends can rub each other the wrong way at times. They can also rally around a member when someone dies or is accused of murder. Danger can come from outside the group as well as within.

All kinds of people do crafts in their spare time. There are those who have made it their profession, but for the vast majority of people, it's an avocation. That throws the field wide open to the kinds of characters a writer can include in their circle of crafters or have as an amateur sleuth: real estate agents, stay-at-home moms and dads, teenagers, those who are retired are all possibilities, but they're not the only ones. Pretty much anyone and any job a writer can think of can be included in a craft-based mystery.

Half the fun of writing these kinds of books is figuring out how to work the craft into the story. The crime could take place at a crafting convention or event. Knowledge of the craft or a skill learned from it could aid in the investigation. A tool used in crafting could be a murder weapon. Glass has sharp edges, knitting needles have points, wood pieces are sometimes heavy and some of the chemicals employed in some crafts can be toxic if used in the wrong way. Possibilities abound.

That doesn't mean that all of the plots in a craft-based cozy need to have the craft front and center with the motive for the killing directly related to it. The craft can be on the periphery. One thing a writer can do is have the crafting community help with the investigation. The group could include people such as retired detectives or lawyers or private investigators who provide advice or information to the amateur sleuth during the course of the investigation. In Nancy Warren's Vampire Knitting Club series, members, all vampires, have hundreds of years of experience and help the main character, a human who inherited a knitting store, solve crimes.

My own books take place in a fictional Los Angeles County beach community. In each book in my series, I highlight events that are peculiar to the beach cities as well as some aspect of decorative painting. Besides finding her painting teacher in her garden, Rory has attended a painting convention where a death occurs and is investigated when someone in her painting group is accused of murder. In one book, a painted piece helped identify a victim of a decades-old crime. In another, a piece provided an important clue to the investigation.

Since cozies are usually written as a series of books, their readers tend to feel a connection to the characters who have become real to them. They enjoy revisiting the world the writer has created to see what happens next to the characters they've come to love. That connection is one thing that gets a reader to pick up the next book in the series. I know that's true for me. One way to build that connection is to show the people in the books doing normal things like crafts. Even those who aren't crafters themselves often have fond memories of a parent or grandparent showing off their skills.

To come up with ideas of how to include decorative painting in a story, I rely on the many years I've been painting. I've taken classes, gone to conventions and read about the craft. What I don't know, I can ask someone about or look up online. But at least I have an inkling of the kinds of things decorative painters do.

That doesn't mean a writer has to do the craft to write about it. A writer can research. I'm not a doctor or a lawyer. That doesn't mean I can't put one in a story. But I think it's a whole lot easier to write about a craft if you've tried it. It adds an air of authenticity.

Whatever the status of the cozy writer, as a reader I expect the details of the craft to be accurate. If they're not and I pick up on it, it takes me out of the story, something every writer does not want to happen. If you do the craft, you're also less likely to have a reader say to themselves, "that's not how it's done."

Another thing that's important is to have the characters do their craft in at least one scene. The main character should be involved somehow since the story revolves around them. Not everyone has to be an expert at it, including the amateur sleuth, but characters should paint or sew or knit or do whatever the featured craft is. People who read these kinds of books generally want to see this. I know I do. As a reader, I feel a little gypped if it's only one scene, but as long as there's at least one, I think it's okay to advertise it as a craft-based cozy.

This is where it can get tough. You want enough of these scenes to satisfy those who do the craft, but not so many that it becomes boring for those who don't. It's a fine line. This is where a beta reader who isn't a crafter and a good editor come in handy. They can tell a writer when there's too much explanation or not enough, where the story slows down, and when there's something they don't understand. It's pretty easy for someone who knows about a craft to use jargon not obvious to the uninitiated.

In my own books, anytime my characters paint, they're either talking about the murder, trying to solve the crime, or something about what they're doing or seeing leads them to a revelation that helps bring the killer to justice.

My favorite review for my first book, *Fatal Brushstroke*, the one with the painting teacher found in Rory's garden, came from Mark Baker who reviews cozies on his Carstairs Considers blog. He's not someone I expected would care about painting, so I was interested to see what he would have to say. The review said in part: "In fact, I found just enough information to make me want to pick up the hobby, which always happens in the best of series. (Now to quickly pick up another book so the desire passes.)" Right there I felt like I'd accomplished one of my goals: to introduce the greater world to decorative painting and showcase how fun it can be. To a certain extent, my books are a love letter to the craft. It also showed me non-painters could enjoy my stories and even want to experience the joy of painting, if only momentarily.

I've tried all sorts of crafts over the years. Some have "stuck," some haven't. I still enjoy finding out about new ones and trying them out on occasion. Reading mysteries set in a crafting world is an easy way to learn. It's also fun to imagine myself doing the craft alongside the characters in a book. I suspect I am not alone in this. I think that's one reason why there are so many craft-based mysteries. For those who do the featured craft, it's a joy to see it acknowledged as being an important part of someone's life. For those who don't, it's fun to read about something new.

There are many kinds of crafts in the world. I keep on hearing about new ones like diamond painting and the revival of old ones like paint-by-numbers. As long as a craft doesn't violate the rules of cozies, which include not featuring explicit sex or violence on the page, I see no reason it can't be the basis of a series. It's up to the writer to use their imagination to figure out how to create stories around it.

Cozy mysteries are filled with ordinary people who find themselves in extraordinary circumstances, compelled to solve a crime that takes place in their close-knit community. That community can easily be one filled with crafters who paint, sew, knit, etc., since these hobbies are often part of the average person's life. This makes the crafting world the perfect setting for a cozy.

Crafts also take patience. So does solving a crime. A crafter spends hours on a project. A detective spends hours knocking on doors and following leads. Crafters also have to learn how to solve problems to fix a project when it goes awry. An amateur sleuth can use the patience and problem-solving skills they've learned while crafting over the years to solve the mystery.

"Cookies open doors"

Food as an Investigative Tool

Maya Corrigan

From Herman Melville's chowder scene in *Moby Dick* to Stanley Tucci's *Taste: My Life Through Food*, writers in various genres describe the aroma, sight, taste, and texture of food to awaken the senses of readers and draw them into the story. Culinary mysteries go beyond simply describing food. By including recipes for the dishes mentioned in their books, culinary cozy writers enable readers to experience the same aromas and tastes as the characters. Food is the centerpiece in my culinary mysteries, defining characters, facilitating sleuthing, and advancing the plot.

Though focused on murder, cozy mysteries affirm the value of family, friends, and community, and in culinary cozies, food brings the characters together. Culinary mysteries have become a larger slice of the cozy market in recent years, mirroring the popularity of cooking shows and food channels. The pandemic forced people indoors and into the kitchen, some of them cooking for the first time. Cooking and eating are comforting routines. They can help us weather a pandemic and make murder more palatable, at least on the page.

My Five-Ingredient Mysteries feature café manager Val and her grandfather solving murders in Bayport, a fictional small town near the Chesapeake Bay. Food proves to be a strong bond between the characters who are two generations apart, though it's a source of tension at first. When Val moves in with Granddad, they are both at a crossroads. She has just broken up with her cheating fiancé and quit her job as a cookbook publicist. After a decade of cooking in a small New York apartment, she is in a happy place, the kitchen where her grandmother taught her to cook. Granddad is not so happy. First, he lost his business. Then his wife died, and recently, his best friend left the neighborhood. Granddad no longer has a role in the life of the town. He sits in front of the TV, watching old movies, and eats only fast and fatty food. Val's mother has asked her to put him on a healthier diet and encourage him to try new activities.

He grumbles about the meals Val makes for him and takes up cooking himself, but he won't try anything with more than five ingredients. Though he sometimes creates havoc in the kitchen, Val is happy that cooking keeps him from being a couch potato. Using her recipes minus a few ingredients, he wangles a position as the local newspaper's recipe columnist, aptly calling himself the Codger Cook. This job gives him the status he craves in the community.

When Val and Granddad become involved in murders, the kitchen is often where they discuss the crime. As they prepare and eat meals together, they share the clues they've picked up and their theories about the murder. While Granddad taps sources in the town where he's lived his whole life, Val gains insights by observing people as they eat. Food is an excellent way to reveal character because people unknowingly reveal their values, fears, obsessions, and aggressions in what and how they eat.

In the fourth Five-Ingredient Mystery, *The Tell-Tale Tarte*, Val watches a suspect dissect a Cornish hen and amass a pile of meat before taking a single bite. That person is disciplined enough to wait for gratification even if it means eating cold food, and, as Val notes, revenge is a dish best served cold. In the third book of the series, *Final Fondue*, Granddad welcomes weekend visitors to the town's tricentennial festival and serves them chocolate fondue. While he remembers the conviviality of fondue parties in the 1970s, his young guests view fondue as a competition and devise ways of hogging the chocolate pot. When an alpha male dips and eats cake cubes so fast that the others can barely get a fork in edgewise, he displays greed, a characteristic of many criminals. A seemingly sweet young woman "accidentally" drops a strawberry into the melted chocolate and goes spear fishing with a fondue fork, keeping everyone else from the chocolate. If she doesn't get her way using passive aggression, Val wonders if the woman might switch to active aggression.

Food doesn't just bring people together and provide a window into their inner lives, it also comforts those dealing with death. Taking food to the grieving is a common practice. It's also an entrée into the murder investigation for an amateur sleuth. While the police have the authority to demand answers from suspects, the culinary mystery's amateur sleuth relies on food to loosen lips. Hence Val's motto: "Cookies open doors." Visiting the murder victim's spouse or other family with a plate of sweets or a dinner casserole gets Val and her grandfather inside a house. Once there, they can slip questions into their condolences and observe the surroundings.

Bookshelves are particularly enlightening. When Val believes a death that the police chalked up to natural causes was really a poisoning, she notes pharmacy textbooks and poison reference books near a suspect's kitchen. Though the suspect, who worked at a poison control center years earlier, had a reason to own such books, "Val was surprised they were so near at hand."

When she and Granddad bring food to an apparently grieving family member, one of them can keep the person talking while the other snoops. Val finds culinary oddities to ponder in the kitchens of suspects. A woman who reportedly rarely cooks has a kitchen with shiny appliances. So why is she wearing an apron in the middle of the afternoon? And why does a suspect who claims a health problem have a pantry full of food that someone with that ailment shouldn't eat?

When the kitchen is the scene of a crime, Val picks up domestic clues, as in this passage from *By Cook or By Crook*, the first Five-Ingredient Mystery: "Next to the doorway where Val stood, the wineglasses in a stemware rack were lined up like troops for inspection. The front two didn't pass muster. Unlike their sparkling comrades, they had water spots suggesting a hasty washing. Crumbs and smears marred the counter between the stemware rack and the fridge. Across the room, though, the granite counter near the sink gleamed. *Someone had cleaned half the kitchen.*" Was that person the victim or the murderer? To understand the crime, Val considers scenarios that explain the spots on the wineglasses and the crumbs on the counter.

As an experienced cook, she has specialized knowledge that the police lack. When she visits the kitchen of man who was found dead a few hours earlier of an apparent heart attack, she notices an open box of chocolates on the table with three pieces missing. "Val leaned down to study the remaining bonbons close up. They had flaws that suggested an amateur candy maker, one who put a bit too much chocolate into the mold and didn't trim the edges after unmolding each piece." It strikes her that such chocolates are perfect vehicles for poison. A would-be poisoner would have to tamper with store-bought chocolates to make them toxic, something the victim might notice and the police surely would. But a killer making homemade bonbons could just mix the poison with the other ingredients.

Val immediately passes on this information to the police chief, a family friend she's known since childhood when Granddad took the younger man under his wing. Whenever Val visits police headquarters, she brings information and baked goods. The combination softens up the chief so he'll answer at least some of her questions. And because he can't abide the sludge that passes for coffee at police stations, he often stops by the café Val manages, giving her a chance to wheedle information from him about the investigation's progress.

Working at the café gives Val other opportunities for sleuthing. Besides her regular patrons who pass on gossip to her, her customers include witnesses, suspects, and occasionally a murderer. She also moonlights as a caterer of small dinner parties. They bring her into contact with people she wouldn't otherwise meet, some of whom air their animosities and disputes at the table. As a caterer, she's nearly invisible to guests while she listens to conversations and observes actions that ultimately lead to a murder solution.

Professional detectives, whether police or Poirot, can question the witnesses and suspects individually or collectively, but it's harder for an amateur sleuth to summon that group. Table scenes solve that problem in culinary mysteries. They bring together people with common interests and murderous tendencies. Table scenes early in my books include the victim who dies either during the meal or shortly afterward as well as the suspects. Later in the book, those initial gatherings are revisited as a way to arrive at the truth. In *Scam Chowder* Granddad orchestrates a re-enactment of a dinner in which one guest went face-first into a bowl of chowder. With Val and a police officer playing the roles of dinner guests, Granddad demonstrates how a person at the table could have poisoned the victim in plain sight without anyone else noticing.

Significant table scenes occur in my fifth book, *S'more Murders*, in which a *Titanic*-obsessed yacht owner hires Val and Granddad to re-create the final meal served on that doomed ship. The dinner guests on the yacht include collectors, dealers, and thieves of *Titanic* memorabilia as well as a descendant of a *Titanic* survivor. Because of a Chesapeake Bay squall, no one finishes the ten-course dinner, and it's the final meal for one person. The same group of people gathers on the yacht for the victim's memorial, catered again by Val and Granddad. The police chief also attends and asks the guests to repeat what they said, heard, and did on the night of the murder. Like a potluck dinner, each person brings something unique to the table, a piece of the puzzle that leads to the revelation of the killer. It takes a community to solve the crime in *S'more Murders*, as befits a cozy mystery.

With a focus on food, culinary mystery writers can skirt a common problem in crime fiction. Because solving a murder involves asking questions of witnesses and suspects, mysteries are necessarily dialogue heavy. To avoid pages of "she said" and "he said," the writer has to include "beats," indicating what characters are doing while talking. What they do in a culinary mystery often relates to food—prepping, cooking, serving, and eating. These actions don't just signal who's talking but also telegraph characters' emotions. In one scene Granddad reacts negatively to Val's theory about the crime as he's cleaning a fish for their dinner: "He scraped the skin and sent translucent scales flipping in all directions." In another scene she's cooking dinner when Granddad informs her that he's set her up with a date. Her annoyance becomes obvious when she flips over a crab cake in the pan and smacks it down so hard that the oil spatters. Usually, cooking generally has a calming effect on Val. Creaming together butter and sugar and mixing in flour puts her in a zone where her mind ranges freely, enabling her to interpret clues and solve puzzles mentally while baking.

Food can also serve as comic relief during the grim task of investigating a murder. In the first few Five-Ingredient Mysteries, Granddad has a lot to learn about cooking. It's not unusual for Val to sniff something burning when she returns home from work. One day she goes into the kitchen to find the oven door open, giving off intense heat, and Granddad scraping splats of half-baked dough off the door. Following her cookie recipe, he'd shaped the dough into balls and spaced them out on a cookie sheet. But he tilted the sheet as he put it into the preheated oven, and the dough balls rolled off. Some of them hang from the oven's center rack like Dali's melting clocks. He accidentally steps on the dough balls that have escaped the oven and grinds them into the floor.

Writing a culinary mystery gives me a chance not just to create kitchen disasters but also to poke fun at aspects of our food culture like the veneration of celebrity chefs. When Chef Henri, who forced Val out of her job in New York, comes to town, he's revealed as a pretentious fake. As Val says, his French accent owes more to the Left Bank of the East River than of the Seine.

Fad diets are another subject that comes up in my mysteries. Val's friend Bethany is a serial fad dieter. She goes on the vampire diet, eating only red food—red meat, berries, and beets. But her craving for oranges and potatoes forces her off the diet. When Bethany's on the caveman diet, Val notes that her friend is aggressive, but she's meeker after switching to the baby food diet, proving that "you are what you eat." Consciously or not, Bethany dresses to match her diet. She wears animal prints while eating like a caveman and pastel frocks with smocking while on the baby food diet. When she goes on the werewolf diet, she explains that she has to fast on the first day of the full moon and "follow some other rules." Val responds, "Like running around the woods and howling?" As weird as Bethany's diets sound, they are actual weight-loss plans touted on blogs and in books.

In writing nine culinary cozies, I've learned that food enriches mysteries in myriad ways. It fleshes out characters, serves as a pretext for sleuthing, and feeds into the investigation for detectives who can interpret culinary clues. Food also adds a dollop of humor to a murder plot. Bon appétit!

Writing the World Around Us

Social Issues in the Cozy

Leslie Budewitz

The modern mystery is a terrific vehicle for exploring social issues because it dives deep into character as well as plot and setting. The mystery hits on the uncomfortable places in life and society; it touches on the rub—where things go wrong and wrongs must be righted.

In this collection, you'll encounter numerous definitions of the cozy mystery. I'm going to give you mine, because it is closely tied to my belief that the cozy can be the perfect forum for addressing social issues.

What is a cozy? The cozy is the ultimate amateur sleuth mystery. The protagonist is an intelligent, independent-minded woman, often emerging from loss or grief. (Of course, men can take on this role, too, but most are women and I write female protagonists, so I'll use "she" and "her" in this essay.) The setting is a defined community, whether a small town, a suburb, or a community within a community, in the urban or city-based cozy. Our protagonist is deeply involved in the community, typically running a business that fosters that sense of connection. When a crime threatens the people and places she loves, she uses her skills, her knowledge, and her relationships to ask questions and make connections that law enforcement can't.

Crime damages the social fabric of a community. While law enforcement is charged with restoring external order by making an arrest and prosecuting, the cozy protagonist restores the social order.

Unlike the protagonists of noir or hard-boiled crime fiction, the cozy protagonist sees the world in a positive light. She believes most people are good and care about each other and that one person can make a difference. She's fully engaged with what's going on around her. So it's only natural that her view of the world will on occasion compel her into action, investigating crime and probing its causes and effects.

Pepper and the Spice Shop Mysteries: My Spice Shop mysteries are set in Seattle's Pike Place Market, a place I fell in love with as a college freshman. It was 1977, just a few years after residents voted to create a historic district and commission to "preserve the Market's physical and unique social character" through public ownership. A non-profit preservation and development authority (PDA) manages day-to-day operations. The PDA's mission is "to preserve, rehabilitate, and protect the Market's buildings; increase farm and food retailing opportunities; incubate and support small and marginal businesses; and provide services for low-income people."

Founded in 1907, the Market includes a year-round farmers' market, two hundred merchants, two hundred arts and craftspeople, and a hundred bars and restaurants, plus five hundred residents and ten million visitors a year—all on nine acres.

It's the perfect place for my Pepper Reece, who bought the Spice Shop after an unexpected divorce and job loss. In her words, she's the poster child for the cliche that life begins at forty. Like many cozy protagonists, she's rebuilding herself and her life while creating new friendships and a new sense of herself.

And yet, everything she's been through makes her exactly the right person to run the shop—and to serve as the Market's unofficial amateur sleuth and problem solver. The cozy protagonist often has an outsider's perspective, whether she's new in town or a local who left and returned, like Erin Murphy in my Food Lovers' Village series, a classic small-town cozy. Pepper is a Seattle native, but she's new to retail and new to working in the Market.

Pepper grew up in a peace and justice house, modeled on the principles of Dorothy Day and the Catholic Worker movement and based on a community I knew as a young lawyer in Seattle. Her parents, a hippie chick and a Vietnam vet, met at a war protest, and they embodied much of the activism of the era. They shared a large, rundown house, called Grace House, with another couple, the parents of Pepper's best friend, Kristen. Grace House was the center of an ever-evolving swirl of activism, from establishing affordable day cares and free meal programs to organizing anti-nuclear rallies. The group disbanded when a trio of members defied the majority and staged a violent protest that went wrong. (The unsolved murder and its consequences are the heart of the cold case investigation in *Killing Thyme*, third in the series.)

But while Pepper's life is deeply rooted in a commitment to community, both she and her brother built careers in the private sector. Pepper sees no contradiction in the daughter of activists marrying a cop; in her view, both are committed to working for the common good, and both can go wrong now and then. (As does their marriage, but her ex's beat includes the Market and their relationship teeters between tense and a truce before settling into a trusted friendship.)

Pepper's career was in HR, working with staff at a large law firm. HR work drew on her natural talents for understanding people and solving problems and gave her skills she uses daily in the shop and dealing with all that the Market throws at her. Those same skills make her a sharp-eyed investigator, keenly aware of the personal impact of crime.

What do I mean by a social issue? I made the deliberate choice to include social issues in the Spice Shop series because they are part of the world I am writing about, a world I love despite its flaws. I could not write honestly about Seattle or food—or about life—without touching on some of the weightier aspects. That is particularly true of the Market, with its history and mission. Of course, social issues arise in small towns and suburbs too, but I don't think I had the confidence or skill to include them when I started the Food Lovers' Village series.

A social issue can be thought of as an external force, an overarching problem of the larger world, that invades a community and harms individuals and relationships. Examples from other cozies are the best illustration. Many current cozy writers were influenced by Diane Mott Davidson, author of the Goldy Schulz catering mysteries. Readers still tell me fondly about discovering her books, one of the first series to incorporate social issues along with a good mystery and recipes. Goldy survived domestic abuse. She's a single mother who runs her own business. In later books, she saves another woman from her own ex, and when her son is a young teen, she takes on school bullying. At about the same time, the late Barbara Neely's groundbreaking Blanche White series shone a light on race and class, through the eyes of a Black woman employed as a housekeeper.

Current authors continue to use social issues to develop character, illuminate setting, and spur plot. In Cleo Coyle's Coffeehouse Mysteries, another single mother probes smuggling, murder disguised as a drug overdose, and a deadly dating app—all while running a business with the ex-husband whose former drug addiction and infidelity still loom over their lives. A subplot in an early book in Barbara Ross's Maine Clambake Mysteries touches on the high cost of prescription drugs; a later plot exposes human trafficking.

The main character in Ellie Alexander's brew pub series grew up in foster care, and her background still influences her. Raquel V. Reyes confronts the subtle, and not-so-subtle, racism her Cuban American protagonist faces in Miami, even from her own mother-in-law. Clashes over environmental issues and property development often crop up in cozies, as in Emmeline Duncan's *Fresh Brewed Murder*, in which the youthful protagonist also tracks down a teen witness and confronts teen homelessness.

These topics can be uncomfortable, even unpleasant. Some readers read for escape. They want to shut out reality for a few hours. I get that. The world is sometimes difficult, especially in recent years. It's a relief to visit a place, on the page, where the pantry is always full and cupcakes are a renewable, calorie-free resource. Authors often get notes from readers thanking us for helping them get through an illness, a time of grief, or a difficult stretch. Does the reader pained by her child's battle with addiction want to read about it?

Maybe not. But what if you're giving her another way to see her own struggles? In showing compassion for characters experiencing a similar crisis, maybe you're giving her hope that other families have come through this, that children can recover and find their way. That was in the back of my mind as I wrote about Aimee, who owns Pepper's favorite vintage shop, and her brother Tony in *Chai Another Day*, and about Hot Dog, a street vendor who gives Pepper the benefit of his experience and a healthy dose of opinion. We first met Hot Dog in *Assault and Pepper*, the series opener, and know that he benefited from the unlikely generosity of an unlikeable man. We've also seen Tony, though we didn't know him by name, when he threw a fit and marched out of a class Pepper was teaching in a program that trains the disadvantaged to work in the food business. Here he's back, struggling, but with a sister who believes in him. Eventually, he succeeds, getting his own place and stable work. Troubles like these look different when we see how a community can pull together to help solve them.

When the cozy protagonist—who is a lot like us, though a little braver—takes on the world and wins, we readers know we can, too. When she talks down a bully, then uses her wits to escape mortal danger, overcome the dark night of the soul, and catch a killer, we're reminded that justice is possible. When cozy characters prevail despite the added pressure that issues like racism and finding reliable childcare bring to the stories, our sense of hope—another key element of the cozy—soars.

As cozy author Raquel V. Reyes says, "The motives behind murder are heavy. Why wouldn't we bring in all the social and economic issues that drive it?"

Writing about these things helps me too. It forces me to stretch. To read more. Listen more. Understand more. To quote another cozy writer, Mary Jane Maffini, "the world is so much more interesting when you know more about the people in it."

So how to write a story that tells the truth, gently? How does a writer use social issues to amplify the other elements of a cozy mystery, to craft a story that shows our main character's strength and her vulnerability, that values community by shining a light on its cracks, that keeps our readers up too late and sends them to bed with a smile? Without preaching, without overwhelming the story, without becoming the story.

As with all fiction, the answer lies in the balance of character, setting, and plot.

Though Pepper chose a different path than her teacher-activist parents, their message that each person has a calling to make the world better is deeply ingrained in her. Now that she's running a retail shop in the Market, a cauldron of human interaction, she gets plenty of opportunities. Not that her determination doesn't sometimes get her into trouble.

In *Assault & Pepper*, Pepper breaks up a spat between two homeless men outside her shop. Later, she finds one of the men dead on her doorstep. Suspicions quickly focus on one of her employees, a young woman reluctant to defend herself. While working to clear her staffer, Pepper develops a friendship with several men who have experienced homelessness. They provide crucial information and help her in other ways. In the process, Pepper—and the reader—delve into some of the problems these men face: Isolation. Mental health struggles. Untreated medical problems. Getting and staying housed. Staying clean and crime-free.

"I am allergic to walls," one man says, a veiled reference to having served time. But it's also an acknowledgment that even those who choose not to live within the typical social constraints are still of value. They are men with stories, who've done bad things and good, who love and are loved. They too are committed to the community. Hot Dog reveals a secret that helps Pepper understand the relationship between her employee and the murder victim. Jim gives her new perspective. And Sam gives her a critical assist when she tackles—literally—the killer, confronting his own fears in the process. Later, he entrusts her with his dog after she helps him reunite with his family.

But Pepper's good intentions don't save her from mistakes. In *Chai Another Day*, Hot Dog forces her to confront her assumptions that she knows what people ought to do. She asks him to help her find Tony, a potential witness to a crime, and convince him to talk to the police. Hot Dog understands why Tony might be reluctant and the potential risks he fears. Pepper does not.

> "Have you seen him since noon Monday?" I asked. His lips tightened and he gripped the plastic ketchup bottle so tight I thought the cap might fly off, ketchup squirting out like a fountain. "I was there when the woman was killed. Upstairs, where a friend lives. I want to know what happened. If he didn't have anything to do with her death, then he has nothing to worry—"
>
> Hot Dog slammed the ketchup bottle on to the counter. Miraculously, the cap stayed on. "You think that on account of you never been in trouble. Oh,

you think you have, 'cause nobody got it easy as it looks from outside. I get that. But real trouble? People itching to take away your life and liberty, never mind the pursuit of happiness? I don't think so."

He disappeared from view, leaving me standing there breathless. Speechless. And apparently clueless [*Chai Another Day*].

Later, Pepper acknowledges her mistake and that she needs her friend's help. Without his willingness to challenge her, and then to cooperate with law enforcement, she would not be able to clear Tony and zero in on the real killer.

It is not possible to write about food in this country without talking about immigration and prejudice. At least, it's not possible for me. In *Chai*, a murder occurs near an Italian restaurant run by a good customer of Pepper's, a Salvadoran immigrant named Edgar. Food crosses cultural lines; a good chef can cook in any style if he's passionate about it and puts in the time. Pepper knows that many back-of-the-house staff are immigrants and wary of the system and that they are not always comfortable speaking English. She's present when the capable but crusty Detective Tracy, who is Black, tells his new young partner, a white man, to go back and interview everyone who works at a particular restaurant again.

"I'm going to need an official interpreter."

Tracy exhaled heavily. "Immigrants? Criminy. Why don't they understand they don't have to be afraid of us?"

Because sometimes they do. "I can call Edgar, and ask him to encourage his kitchen staff to cooperate" [*Chai Another Day*].

Pepper sees both sides of the problem and uses her connection to the witnesses to find a solution.

When Pepper walks down the street with her friend Seetha, who is of South Asian ancestry, a man verbally attacks Seetha. A self-described "standard-issue white woman," Pepper wants Seetha to confront the behavior or at least report it. She doesn't realize that Seetha's choice to carry on, refusing to let the abuse define her or disrupt her routine, is itself an act of defiance. And that constantly confronting ugliness is exhausting. But she learns.

No question, these topics can get heavy. That's one reason why social issues are often best placed in backstory and subplots and handled with a light touch.

In 2021, as the country was still struggling with Covid-19 and its personal and economic fallout, I started the sixth book, a Christmas mystery called *Peppermint Barked*. I'd heard other cozy authors say they didn't intend to write about the pandemic, that readers wouldn't want to read about it and that it didn't belong in their cozy worlds. But I quickly realized I could not continue to write authentically about the Market if I didn't touch on an experience that dramatically affected everyone in the country. That meant I had to balance the risk of making the reader uncomfortable with the desire to portray the impact on my story world. An added challenge: I was writing in 2021 for publication in July 2022. Was I even going to be able to get it right?

Covid is not a central theme. It's in the background, a fact of life. This is the first Christmas with the Market fully open again. Shoppers are excited. Decorations are in full bloom. Moods are bright and wallets are open. But some stores have closed, and a death created a vacant space next to Pepper's pal Vinny's wine shop, a space at the center of a deadly conflict. I also wanted to show how the pandemic had been a positive stressor for Pepper's shop, as it was for real-life grocers and food retailers. More people were cooking at home, learning new skills, and trying new recipes. Pepper and her crew pivoted, expanding their mail-order business. Now, she's got to plot the next steps. Using the pandemic allowed me to highlight the economic fragility of small businesses. It also gave me threads to follow in *Peppermint Barked* and future books, including the staffing shortage and the impact of a trusted employee's departure. And I was able to show a close-knit staff growing even closer, after what they've all been through together.

Subplots often mirror or echo the main plot, giving the reader a slightly different perspective, a variation on a theme. Or they may expand on some aspect of character. In *Guilty as Cinnamon*, second in the series, Pepper discovers that two men she knows from the bar and restaurant they run helped a female co-worker escape domestic abuse. They also ran an unsavory financial scheme that destroyed a business. Can their good deed outweigh the harm they did? What about the danger one of them fears the former co-worker now presents, because she knows too much about their past?

And in the end…. Even when we read for entertainment or escape, we want an emotional experience. We want to savor that food with the characters, participate in their conversations, worry, laugh, cry, and celebrate with them. We want to visit a place we've never been or revisit one that's familiar. We want a believable mystery that makes us think and feel.

For me, a good cozy does what all good fiction does: It shows us something about the world around us, while keeping us turning the pages. A protagonist engaged with her community will inevitably face social issues. We're writing about people, after all, and people are social. People have issues. One reason I love writing and reading cozies is their flexibility. They can be contemporary or historical. They can open cold cases or probe new crimes. They can take us to small towns, suburbs, or big cities. And everywhere our cozy protagonist goes, with every crime she solves, she reminds us that despite all its challenges, and sometimes because of them, this world is worth loving.

Cultural Elements Elevate
a Cozy Mystery

Jennifer J. Chow

The allure of a cozy mystery is in part due to its familiarity. A typical setting for a "cozy" is a small town or village with a wonderful (if somewhat quirky) cast of characters. The protagonist is an amateur sleuth who is usually relatable to the reader—an everyday individual who solves cases that the official police force finds baffling. A cozy mystery wraps you in comfort through its recognizable aspects. Culture can play a huge role in creating that necessary sense of connection, and I believe that emphasizing cultural elements is particularly relevant in today's world and to modern readers.

I devoured cozy mysteries while growing up, mostly due to their charm. I liked being transported and whisked away to the English countryside to enjoy the sweetness of a tight-knit community. Besides the unrecognizable geography of the mysteries I read, I soon realized I didn't have much in common with the main character's heritage. None of them reflected my own Asian background. This realization made me feel unwelcome on a heart-wrenchingly personal level. As a reader, it also pulled me out of the story and lowered my enthusiasm for the novel.

Who I am is shaped by my culture, which informs my perspective on life. Cultural identity influences viewpoints in real life, and that truism can be extended to the fictional realm. The point of a *contemporary* cozy mystery is to reflect the world around us. To make a mystery ring true in modern times, it should mirror today's diversity and provide characters with relatable cultural identities.

Personally, I try to incorporate my heritage into my own writing. In my Sassy Cat Mysteries, the protagonist, Mimi Lee, is biracial. She has a Caucasian father and a Malaysian Chinese mother. (Likewise, my own father is Malaysian Chinese.)

96

The first book in that series is called *Mimi Lee Gets a Clue*. This title works on multiple levels because (a) Mimi is trying to track down physical clues for the investigation; (b) she's still puzzling out her own purpose in life as a twenty-five-year-old; and (c) she's trying to understand her layered identity.

Sometimes being of mixed race is helpful to Mimi as an amateur sleuth. She's free to pass into places like the exclusive country club where her dad is a member, which helps with her detecting. She's also able to navigate dual worlds because of her background. For example, she can easily connect to a young female entrepreneur of South Asian descent one moment and then attend a fancy charity gala with powerful Hollywood types in a subsequent scene.

Other times, being biracial proves to be a disruption to her sleuthing practices. This can happen in a minor and humorous way, such as when her mom becomes fixated on matchmaking and securing an ideal partner for Mimi. Mimi's mother herself married young and then moved to the States, so she pins her hopes on relationships, causing her to brainstorm (disastrous) dating scenarios for her daughters. Mimi has experienced things like questionable relationship apps, superpowered speed dating, and awkward set-ups with take-out delivery boys. Sometimes Mimi feels caught between the two cultures of her particular background, like during a special occasion. For the celebration, she takes extra time debating on whether to wear a qipao or a kebaya since she wants to honor both parts of her mother's Malaysian Chinese ancestry.

Then there are the moments when Mimi believes she's a total outsider. She feels like she can't be accepted for her own unique identity. Mimi sometimes struggles with navigating America as a person of mixed race. She senses that she's either too Asian or not Asian enough, depending on whom she's interacting with, and has to straddle a frustrating line. In an emotional moment for her, Mimi gets called a "hollow bamboo" by her mother's acquaintance. This phrase signifies that Mimi is seen as an Asian American with no true substance inside of her.

Usually, though, Mimi embraces her identity and forges her own path. She deliberately tries to reject her mother's superstitious ways. In one scene, her mother cries "Alamak!" in shock because Mimi wants to live in an apartment with an unlucky unit number. Mimi is more than happy residing in the space, though, particularly since she has a new cute lawyer neighbor. She also fights against her mother's mindset of predetermined fate by taking destiny into her own hands. Mimi does not wait for situations to resolve by themselves. When she (or her friends or family) is accused of a crime, she's willing to sleuth at all hours and in potentially dangerous places, with only her trusty telepathic sassy cat by her side.

Identity and culture are also prevalent themes in my newest series, the L.A. Night Market Mysteries. All the novels take place against the backdrop of the local night market. Night markets are an authentic tie-in to my own experiences in East Asia. These evening open-air fairs full of shopping and eating enticements also allow for a mysterious and exciting venue where a murder might take place.

The L.A. Night Market novels feature two cousins who run a food stall. Yale Yee is a second-generation Chinese American, and her cousin, Celine Yee, newly arrived in the United States, comes from a moneyed existence in Hong Kong. Book One in the series is called *Death by Bubble Tea*. As a culinary cozy, the novel is part of a subgenre focused on food. In typical cozy style, the L.A. Night Market Mysteries also provide unique recipes at the back of the books as a bonus.

Distinctive meals and snacks are tangible ways of representing and showing culture. In fact, food is a primary love language for Yale's father (a dim sum restaurant owner), who is not prone to emoting through hugs or other physically demonstrative gestures. Moreover, the titular bubble tea drink is central to the book's plot and holds a clue to the culprit.

Yale's father, affectionately called Ba, has passed on to Yale the principles that "relationships are the essential heartbeats of life" and that "family should be together." There is an understood obligation to support relatives no matter the cost. Yale and Celine are polar opposites in personality (bookish versus extroverted, respectively). Even so, Yale feels duty-bound to work side by side with her cousin in running the food stall—and then later, to partner together in solving a murder case.

Trouble comes when Yale literally stumbles over a dead body, and the food stall's signature bubble tea drink is found near the victim. Family is important and now the two Yee cousins are thrown under police suspicion. Internal conflict arises within Yale because she has a strong instilled sense of respect for authority. She figures she should let the police handle things, and yet Yale feels compelled to rescue her family and erase the accusation. Furthermore, Yale is drawn to this specific case because the murder victim culturally resonates with her. They hail from the same ethnic background, speak a common dialect, and even gravitate toward similar feng shui concepts.

Celine, on the other hand, puts herself first in situations as a general rule, even if it means hindering a homicide investigation. At one point, she insists on going shopping instead of handing over helpful evidence to the detective in charge. She also believes any problem will go away if you throw enough money at the issue.

Celine's outlook and spontaneity often clashes with Yale's reserved personality. However, they both come together over two important cultural concepts: saving face and filial piety. The cousins don't want the Yee name to get dragged through the mud, for embarrassment to come to the family. Since the food stall is connected to Yale's father, a beloved elder, they also don't want him or his restaurant business to be negatively affected. The cousins decide to pair up to use their different methods of sleuthing (Yale: bookish research; Celine: social media savvy) to figure out the killer. On a lighter note, they're also willing to use bribes in the case … but in varying ways. Celine lures with cash while Yale opts for food bribes to help eyewitnesses share more and make suspects divulge their secrets.

In Book Two of the series, *Hot Pot Murder*, a cultural food is again at the heart of the story. Too bad someone dies during the special feast which features meats and veggies dipped into boiling broth. The special meal has been organized for the local Asian American restaurant owners, so culture does play a large role in this specific plot. In the book, assumptions are made based on the shared Asian roots of the suspects. However, these conjectures might or might not be relevant or reliable. In *Hot Pot Murder*, the cousins also use their upbringing to spot clues in more hidden places, like through a written Chinese character.

With the L.A. Night Market Mysteries, I love how the cousins share similar backgrounds while also displaying differences. The complexities of the two characters indicate that subtle variations can be mined even from a single culture.

Much-needed diverse tales ground us in the truth of the modern world. At the same time, they hopefully increase reader empathy and excitement. Complex characters with personalized cultural backgrounds lead to richer stories. Multidimensional individuals elevate a mystery to go beyond a plain whodunit. In fact, this diversity of characters and realistic personalities will serve to enhance the entire cozy mystery genre.

PART THREE

Writing Setting

Mise-en-Scène

Rabbi Ilene Schneider

Mise en scène, literally the setting of a scene, when used for stagecraft refers to what the audience sees—the set design, props, lighting, positioning of the actors, costumes, makeup. In cinema, the term describes everything within the frame of the camera, including all the elements used in stage productions, plus location, atmosphere, film stock, weather, camera angles, depth of field, soundtrack. But can the phrase be used to describe the written medium? Yes, but with inherent difficulties not faced by creators of the visual arts of live theater, movies, and television.

In the visual arts, we use our eyes. In the written medium, we use our imaginations. When we attend a stage show or watch a movie, we see how the production designers and directors, costumers and makeup artists, lighting engineers and sound technicians envision the scene, and how their interpretations influence the story telling. But authors of books, whether fiction or nonfiction, have to rely on their words to set the scenes: the atmosphere; the look and feel of the location; the appearance, dress, accents, tone of voice of the characters. "Show, don't tell" is the essence of script writing, whether for live plays or filmed ones, but it is almost the antithesis—and certainly the challenge—of book writing.

Wuthering Heights would tell a different story if set on a warm, sunny beach; the gloominess of the fog on the moors in both the book and the movie versions heightens the helplessness of the tortured and doomed relationship of Catherine and Heathcliff. But in the book, Emily Brontë had to rely on the written word to describe the couple's despair, leaving the visualization to the interpretation of the individual readers' imagination, while the movie broadcasts it, pun intended, to the audience.

Would the movie version of Graham Greene's *The Third Man* have been so hauntingly and successfully suspenseful without the alternately jaunty and melancholy zither music in the soundtrack? Would *Citizen Kane* be acclaimed as the best movie ever made if it weren't for Orson

Welles' innovative use of camera angles and shadows? Would *Phantom of the Opera* have the same impact without the crashing of the chandelier or *Miss Saigon* without the on-stage helicopter? Would the tension and visceral fear so essential to *Jaws* be as great without the familiarity of the location to anyone who has gone to a public beach on the East Coast—not to mention the menacing thumping of the soundtrack? In these and so many other movies and plays, the visual and auditory images enhance and even forward the plot.

How do authors decide not only where to set the plot of a book, specifically a cozy mystery, but also how they can describe the location vividly enough to engage the imaginations of the readers? As we will see, the setting of a book can become an essential element of a cozy and even be part of the plot, for example, in locked-room mysteries. Yet first, we need to examine some defining characteristics of a cozy. Why is it considered its own category of the mystery genre, separate from traditional, police procedural, thriller, psychological suspense, noir and other subgenres of the umbrella mystery category?

I once heard a cozy defined as a book you can read in bed before going to sleep—and still fall asleep. There's no gratuitous or explicit sex, no blatant gore or violence on the page. It's all behind the scenes. There is also no obscene language, although that "rule" has loosened a bit. Many authors and fans accept as a cozy a book into which an occasional expletive-deleted has crept, as long as it is appropriate to the circumstances and isn't overused. For example, in the first book of my Rabbi Aviva Cohen Mysteries, *Chanukah Guilt*, my protagonist, Rabbi Cohen, wakes up in a hospital bed after her car has been forced off the road and into a tree. "I opened my eyes to see a blurry shape sitting next to my bed and another blurry one hovering nearby. I tried to fumble around where I thought the night table would be, but one shoulder hurt and the other arm had something attached to it. 'Where the fuck are my glasses?'"

"A familiar voice coming from the seated figure said wryly, 'She's fine.'"

Police procedurals can be traditionals, as long as they do not have explicit sex, violence, or language; if they do, they are usually grouped with thrillers or noir (U.S. or British or Scandinavian) or psychological suspense or combinations, but those others are never cozies nor traditionals.

Humor is another feature of many mysteries, particularly of cozies and, less often, traditionals. The titles of many if not most cozies contain puns. Mine are *Chanukah Guilt*, *Unleavened Dead*, *Yom Killer*, and the work-in-progress *Killah Megillah*. Future titles include suggestions from friends: *Shavuot Shootout*, *Simchat Trauma*, *Hoshana Robbery*, *Simchat Horror*, *Tu Were Shot*, *Shabbat Whine*, *Jewish Prudence*, *Hava Na'killer*, *Gefilte by Association*.

Cozies and traditionals have a lot of overlapping characteristics, namely keeping sex and violence off the page and in the background, no matter how integral they are to the plot. So what is it that sets the two apart? There is one major difference: the protagonist of a traditional mystery, whether an omniscient third-person narrator or a first-person one, is a professional law enforcement official or private detective, but the protagonist of a cozy mystery is an amateur sleuth. Always. No exceptions. There are two classic mystery series that are perfect illustrations of the difference between the subgenres: Agatha Christie's books featuring Hercule Poirot are traditional mysteries; those featuring Miss Marple are cozies.

Another stereotypical difference, but definitely not a defining one, is amateur sleuths are usually female and professionals are usually male, as are their creators. But ever since Sara Paretsky introduced us to V.I. Warshowski and Sue Grafton to Kinsey Millhone, there have been as many Detective Inspector Vera Stanhopes as there are Detective Inspector Jimmy Perezes; as many Detective Chief Inspector Jane Tennisons as Detective Chief Inspector Morses. Note, however, that these examples are professionals (and, only incidentally, British). It is not as easy to find male amateur sleuths or even male cozy authors. In fact, I can think of only three cozy series with protagonists who are male amateur sleuths, all written by male authors: the Aaron Tucker Mysteries and the Comedy Tonight Series, both by Jeff Cohen; the Geezer-Lit Mystery Series, by Mike Befeler; and the Pot Thief Mysteries, by J. Michael Orenduff.

It should also be noted that there are some who use "cozy noir" as a category for cozies that do include some relatively mild violence or scatology, whether in language or a relationship. I would include Jeff Markowitz's *Death and White Diamonds* as a cozy noir. His protagonist is a male amateur sleuth and the setting is a non-metropolitan coastal area (cf. below). It is difficult to describe the book as a cozy, though, when it includes a scene using a chum cannon to unsuccessfully dispose of a body. It's very funny if you're a fan of dark humor, but more noir than cozy. (Both Jeffs are from Central Jersey, but I suspect it's coincidental, not causal.)

The amateur sleuth, however, needs to have access to the police, which is why so many of them are romantically involved with police officers or private detectives. They hope they can work cooperatively with their law enforcement official/significant other, in the often naïve expectation the professionals will impart important clues to them. But they wouldn't be very ethical professionals if they divulged classified information to civilians and potentially compromised the investigation or caused the case to be thrown out of court. Instead, the law enforcement officials often consider their significant other/amateur sleuth as interfering and obstructionist and in need of protection and rescue. Amateur sleuths have tenacity, imagination, intuition, curiosity, recklessness, impulsivity, zealousness, and determination to see justice done, not to mention incredible luck in staying alive despite their recklessness and impulsivity. What they don't have is the kind of accessibility to computer databases and forensics reports and arrest reports and the entrée to certain locations and witnesses that the police do. Yet, despite this lack of resources, amateurs do tend to be successful in solving cases that stymie professionals because they do have access to gossip and innuendo and clues the police may overlook.

Setting can be one of the defining characteristics differentiating cozies from traditionals. Cozies are almost always set in suburban, rural, or isolated areas but seldom in urban ones. Traditionals are often in urban settings, but are also common in suburban, rural, or isolated ones (such as the above-mentioned coastal area). An amateur sleuth needs to be able to have easy access to suspects and witnesses, needs to be familiar with a location, and needs to understand the societal norms and customs of an area.

When a cozy is set in an urban area, it is usually in a close-knit neighborhood or a small, often ethnic, enclave, such as Naomi Hirahara's Japantown Mysteries, which take place mostly in Chicago and in Los Angeles, but in neighborhoods populated by Japanese Americans who were interned during World War II. Other settings for cozies in urban settings are in specific "closed" institutions, such as a library, a theater (live or movie), a mom-and-pop store, an independent bookstore, a café, a gift shop, or a boutique. Elaine Viets' Dead-End Job Mysteries, set in Fort Lauderdale, are a good example. Fort Lauderdale's population isn't in the same league as New York City's or even Miami's, but it is a city, complete with a large international airport, downtown, cruise port, separate neighborhoods and suburbs, and gridlocked traffic. Viets' protagonist, though, finds jobs in small businesses which have a "cozy" feel, limited characters, and a small pool of suspects.

Another aspect of the amateur sleuth's influence on the choice of location is she (as noted above, the protagonist of a cozy is usually female) is often an independent entrepreneur, running her own craft shop, bakery, café, catering company, real estate agency, RV camp, blacksmith shop … the list is as endless as the authors' imaginations. In addition, whether they are divorced, widowed, single, or happily (or unhappily) married to law enforcement officials or to civilians, many have children, yet somehow manage to juggle childcare, school activities, home life, and sleuthing. They are often under forty and fit.

Lately, there have been more protagonists who are older women, often retired, living in senior facilities, with a close group of female and male friends eager to assist them in their sleuthing and adult children living elsewhere. Mike Befeler's above-mentioned Geezer-Lit Mysteries feature an older male who has the added burden of short-term memory loss.

My own protagonist is in between these two ends of the range. She is a rabbi, rapidly approaching sixty, twice divorced, with no children, cares more for comfort than fashion, goes to a hair salon as seldom as possible, and is pathologically exercise-avoidant. But she does live in a small town, site of a state university and on the edge of the New Jersey Pine Barrens. And she does have an "in" with the local police—her first ex-husband, whose romantic interest she is not sharing, is the interim police chief.

There are several other factors that help authors choose their settings for a cozy mystery. The ubiquitous "they" say to write what you know, so a lot depends on what kind of location the author is familiar with. I would not recommend, for example, that a Bostonian set her book in a suburb of Billings, Montana, unless she has lived there or visited often. Of course, it is possible to create a fictitious location, but it won't feel authentic unless it is near a real place.

Authors need to consider, too, how much time they want to spend on researching an unfamiliar location, even a fictitious one situated near a real one. One can create a mystery in a non-existent small town along the Chesapeake Bay, for example, but should know whether a real store in a nearby neighborhood the protagonist is shopping at is open late at night. I guarantee the readers will know. They will also know what the sales tax is, that New Jersey does not have self-service gas stations, which high schools are rivals, the names of the pro sports teams and their records, and which major roads lead where. The afore-referenced Jeff Cohen once wrote that his protagonist was driving down the Garden State Parkway and looked out the car window at Camden. The problem is that Camden is about sixty miles from the Garden State Parkway. When I called him on it, his response was "That's why it's called fiction." I quote him frequently.

My books are set in a fictitious town in South Jersey, which is where I live. One is set in a fictitious suburb of Boston, where I grew up (as did my protagonist). I know both areas well enough to make references to real places. At the same time, however, I am careful to disguise my pretend locations (and characters) enough for "plausible deniability" in case people I know think I am basing events or people on them. But neighbors and other friends living in my town have commented on the kick they get out of recognizing familiar locations.

Another factor in determining a location is whether it fits the needs of the plot and the personality or job of the protagonist. Obviously, a charter boat operator is not going to live in the desert, but someone who has always lived in a desert could inherit such a company from an uncle. Said protagonist, who is looking for a change in her life (or running from an abusive relationship or disastrous divorce, both of which circumstances can lead perilously close to the thriller or psychological suspense genres), decides to run the company instead of selling it and becomes the stereotypical and possibly humorous fish out of water (or, in this case, fish in water).

The setting can be important to the narrative. It can heighten the sense of dread or menace, or even be crucial to the plot. A closed room mystery is best when set in an isolated mansion. A sudden death at a school reunion is more suspenseful when taking place on an island—during a hurricane. A college campus can take on the features of a small town, complete with nosey and noisy neighbors, work-life balance issues, financial problems, romantic entanglements, jealousies, drug and alcohol abuse, a close-knit or alienating environment, welcoming or hostile surroundings.

Exotic locales—exotic to those who don't live there—present another challenge. If the author is intimately familiar with the location, the difficulty of authenticity and burden of research are lessened. It is too easy, though, for authors to be so focused on portraying the milieu, its flora, fauna, topography, weather, and other characteristics that they indulge in "info dumps" at the expense of the pacing of the plot. I once read a traditional police procedural in which the state trooper described so many details of the surroundings that the plot was basically ignored; there was little police work done and the ending was rushed, with the criminal confessing before dying of a heart attack at the trooper's feet. While it can be a challenge to balance the right amount of description to create atmosphere without becoming a travelogue, it cannot be done at the detriment of the plot. The best and smoothest solution for info dumps, whether describing the background of a locale or a character, is to break the descriptions into smaller scenes and weave them throughout the narrative.

So, yes, mise en scène is equally important for the written medium as it is for the visual arts, even if trickier to accomplish. Just remember: it doesn't have to be accurate, but it has to be plausible.

Handling Diverse Settings

Marni Graff

The first time I visited England decades ago, I stepped off the plane and felt like I was coming home. Despite being a native Long Islander, I've always been drawn to the United Kingdom, with many of the books I read British crime novels. Friends knew not to call me Sunday nights when *Masterpiece Mystery* was on.

Years later, winding down a nursing career where I studied writing and wrote for journals and magazines, I planned to finally write full time, and chose mystery novels, as that was what I like to read the most. An offer came to spend a summer studying Gothic literature at Exeter College in Oxford, the town of Inspector Morse, where I'd dig deeply into Wilkie Collins and Daphne du Maurier, two of my favorite authors. Oxford was a place I longed to visit, and it lived up to every expectation I'd held, from the ancient architecture and glowing golden stone buildings to its reverence for learning. I took the pledge to read in the Radcliffe Camera and was able to review Collins' original broadsheets for *The Woman in White*. It was a magical experience and solidified my decision to set a crime series in England, even as I knew setting it there would be a challenge. Why set a series in a place I don't live in? How would I handle all of the questions that would arise long distance?

On some level, I suppose I had a desire to live in England which would be satisfied through my protagonist. Placing my series in the UK, I rationalized, would give me the perfect excuse for frequent setting research trips. Nursing had taught me to plan ahead and be organized, and I reasoned I could apply those same things to my research trips. That summer I only knew my main character would be an American journalist I named Nora Tierney, who lived in England and had to learn the differences in culture and language, a mild fish-out-of-water experience. She would use her nosiness to become involved in solving a murder investigation to clear her best friend of a murder charge. I brought a notebook to sketch out details as I fleshed out the bones of that first novel and prepared for Oxford to work its magic. I would be the sponge Neil Simon says every writer must be at heart, soaking up atmosphere and the way people conversed and acted toward each other, while my imagination created my own world and its characters.

The Blue Virgin, a metaphor for the murder victim, is set in Oxford and drew from my time there as I absorbed the mix of town and gown that so frustrated Morse, an Oxford dropout. I took countless photographs and gathered postcards, maps, and tourist brochures to keep my impressions accurate when I returned home and plunged into writing the book. I developed a friendship with another mature Oxford student who lives in Bath who agreed to be a contact for me and became a great friend. Helen continues to help on any book set near an area she knows. I also visited St. Aldates, the Oxford station for the Thames Valley Constabulary, which housed the CID office of the detective on that case. For the offer of having that person's name mentioned in the acknowledgments of the eventual book, I found a detective willing to answer questions via email as they arose when I was home writing. He gave me small details of the station and its workings that added to the real feel of the station when Nora's best friend is arrested.

That continues to be the case for me, seven books and two series later. After a visit to the locale, I look for a local contact in the area where each book will be set. To date, I've never had a person I've asked to answer questions via email turn me down once they learn they will be thanked in the subsequent book. This can often be someone from the police, a wealth of information, but also can be someone who lives in the area and can tell me about life there, often giving me a nugget of information not readily available to tourists.

My anticipation that setting a series in the UK would mean justification for trips back has proven to be true, Covid notwithstanding. I am usually in some part of the UK every other year, far ahead of a planned book. My next visit will revisit Cornwall but will hopefully include time in Wales and Scotland, more than my previous cursory stops allowed, for future novels. Visiting in person stimulates my creativity when exploring a new vicinity that I find exciting, and I hope that translates to my eventual readers.

That became the hallmark of my process for my UK-set books: an in-person visit to an area where I gather information well ahead of the writing, and more importantly, absorb not just the sights but also the smells and sounds and *feel* of that particular area. I would find it difficult to use Google alone to place a book in a country I hadn't visited, although it certainly can be done, and I do use Google and Google Earth as an adjunct when questions arise once I'm home and writing. But for me, the experience of being in a particular locale adds to my ability to bring it to life. I believe setting is a character in a novel; it's the stage I move my characters around, and readers need to be able to picture themselves there. That's what I do when I read a book, and I choose to believe my readers agree.

In my acknowledgments I explain to readers what is fictional and what is real. Yes, you can have high tea in Oxford at Nora's favorite place, The Old Parsonage, but no, you won't find her new house behind it. I've sited that on what is The Old Parsonage's back garden. Similarly, in *The Evening's Amethyst*, St. Giles Church is where I've said it is, next to Nora's fictional cottage, complete with its crooked sidewalk and old tombstones. But there is no rectory that houses the young vicar, her husband, and son who become Nora's neighbors. I needed a playmate for Nora's own young son, and people she would add to her community of supporters since her mother and stepfather are back in America.

I was also wary of keeping Nora in one town in the UK, in an effort to avoid what I call the Jessica Fletcher trap. How many murders can one small town hold? There are five books published in *The Nora Tierney English Mysteries* so far, and they've been set in Oxford, twice in the Lake District, Bath, and back to Oxford. Book six will be set in Cornwall. I find moving Nora around means readers are able to travel to these places too and don't feel as if they are reading the same book over and over.

It's easy to invent a reason for Nora to visit a new area. For instance, she's moved on to write children's books, and in *The Golden Hour*, Book Four in the series, Nora's in Bath staying with a friend for a presentation at a real bookstore, Mr. B's Emporium of Reading Delights. Remember my Bath contact? Nora stays at Helen's real bed and breakfast, Hill House. Helen was of course a delightful resource when I stayed with her to explore Bath, not only for the bookstore where she'd arranged an interview but also for taking me to nearby Victoria Park, which ended up being used in an important scene in the book.

Grounding Nora in (mostly) real places any reader could visit adds to the verisimilitude I try to achieve. For Mr. B's, I visited him and the bookstore, had a tour with the owner, took interior and exterior photos of the shop, and garnered his permission to use the site for Nora's book event. When I assured him no one would be murdered there, he seemed disappointed and told me, "Could do, though," if my plans changed. He sells *The Golden Hour* proudly at his shop.

In order to keep a sense of community that plays an essential role in any mystery, I've added several recurring characters who stay in contact with Nora. One is her best friend, Val Rogan, whose arrest starts the action of the first book. Val continues to appear in each subsequent Nora book, a trusted friend Nora calls, texts, or visits in person. Val helped Nora find her Oxford home and is her son's godmother.

When Nora moves temporarily to the Lake District for a year, she lives with the illustrator of her children's books, Simon Ramsey, at the lodge he and his sister run. Simon is another character who appears in different ways in each book, his role increasing and decreasing according to the needs of the story. In *The Scarlet Wench*, a theater troupe arrive at Ramsey Lodge to stage Noël Coward's play *Blithe Spirit* when a storm leaves the cast temporarily stranded at the lodge and an actor is murdered. Besides having tremendous ramifications for Simon's business, Nora is anxious to help find the culprit to remove the danger of having a murderer on site as she has an infant son by that time. Since so much of the action revolves around the interior of the lodge, I included a drawing of the room layout on the second floor where the cast is housed.

With chapter epigrams all lines from the actual play, I had to approach Coward's estate to obtain permission to reproduce that many lines, which they gave me for a very modest fee on the condition I would send them a copy of the finished book for his archives, which I was thrilled to do. That was a case where Gmail came heavily into play, as all of my correspondence with Coward's estate lawyers was online.

That first Oxford trip coincided with a time I was writing interview articles for *Mystery Review* magazine, where I'd been fortunate to interview and learn from wonderful crime authors whose books I read and enjoyed, such as Val McDermid, Ian Rankin, and Deborah Crombie. When my editor learned I was traveling to Oxford, she asked if I would consider training to London one day to interview P.D. James at her London townhouse. The queen of contemporary British mystery was my hero when it came to modern crime novels, and I could scarcely believe my good fortune. That day began a friendship and mentorship that lasted the last fifteen years of the baroness's life. James had been a huge influence on my writing, along with the Golden Agers I'd gobbled up as a young reader—Christie, Sayers, Marsh, Tey, Allingham. Her strong use of setting matched my own vision, while her depth of characterization floored me. James was gracious and kind, generous and warm, with a wicked sense of humor.

Here is where happenstance comes in, which every writer needs to keep in mind. I'd reveled in just being in the company of someone whose work I admired, and once the more formal interview had been accomplished, James asked if I'd like a coffee in her ground floor kitchen. We sat around the table where I knew she wrote her first drafts in longhand after exhaustive outlines, and our casual talk turned to my nursing career. She had many questions for me when she learned the position I would shortly leave was as a medical consultant for a New York movie studio, aiding actors and directors to bring as much reality as possible to the dialogue and action of medical scenes. I was a regular on the soap opera *One Life to Live* and worked on *Law & Order* too.

James extracted an oath from me before I left her that day, that once I'd written several of my planned English mysteries, I'd start a second series featuring a nurse who did my consulting work. "Readers love a behind-the-scenes look at a job they don't know," she insisted. "Promise me one day you'll write a mystery that revolves around someone who does that job." A few years later I started *The Trudy Genova Manhattan Mysteries*, and dedicated the first, *Death Unscripted*, to James.

Growing up near New York City meant I knew that setting well, yet I lived in North Carolina by this time, so I still arranged a contact for police matters and have remained friends with an actress from the soap opera who verifies my ideas about the business end of things from the cast's point of view. Shops and their owners change frequently, and she can talk to those changes too. What doesn't change are the sites of landmarks like Lincoln Center, just up the street from the studio where Trudy is based, where the first book is set. And yet, as I was wary of bogging her down in one place, the second book in the Trudy series, *Death at the Dakota*, takes place at the Victorian apartment complex that more modern readers will remember as the site of John Lennon's death. His widow, Yoko Ono, still lives there, and as Trudy gets on an elevator Ono gets off. A marvel when it was built, the Dakota continues to be a storied condominium residence for New York's wealthiest and in the past was the home of many celebrities such as Lauren Bacall, Judy Garland, and Rudolf Nureyev. In reality, the Dakota does not allow filming inside (the interiors for *Rosemary's Baby* were all sets), but in Trudy's world it does. Coming across the room plans for the apartment Leonard Bernstein and his family once owned allowed me to use it as the setting for Trudy's medic role on a made-for-television movie. I included those in the front of that book, too, so readers could follow the action when she's on set.

At the end of this second Trudy book, she asks the NYPD detective she's started dating, Ned O'Malley, if he would travel with her to her childhood home to investigate the death of her father twelve years before. That little nugget was planted in book one, with Trudy convinced her father's accident was a case of murder. *Death in the Orchard* is the book in progress, and it takes place in Schoharie, New York, at Trudy's family home on the apple orchard her older brothers run. Having a son who once lived in Schoharie made that an easy choice for her home setting as I'd visited the town often, a factor also planted in book one. A local resident is my current contact and answers email questions. She'll also be a beta reader for the book, to pick up any errors I've made.

That brings me to the idea of a series arc. I start each book with the ending: who is the victim, and why did they have to die, taking into account the chosen setting and why that person is there, and then the identity of the murderer, too, if it's a whodunit. Only once, in *The Golden Hour*, did I write a can-they-stop-him where the reader knew the identity of the antagonist up front.

I then work my way toward that end goal, placing suspects and clues, adding in red herrings along the way, allowing for changes and subplots as I write. Each mystery is solved in a book, with some kind of resolution, but the arc I'm talking about refers to Nora or Trudy as characters. I need to show growth in their characterizations, and so those were the jottings I made when designing each arc. As their personal lives change, so will their circumstances. I have brief notes for the personal lives for six books in the Nora series and four for Trudy. I'll see once those are written if I have any more to say for each woman. While the alternate main point of view is the police procedural investigation, it's clear that Nora and Trudy are the main protagonists of each series, no matter where I take them.

One other thing about a series arc: I have tremendous respect for the police and their difficult work, which is why I take such pains to make that point of view accurate. I picture the women's relationship with each detective in their respective series as more in the form of Nora or Trudy insisting she can be of help to them and then having to prove that. For instance, when we first meet Oxford detective Declan Barnes in the Nora series, she frustrates him with this attitude, as well as her journalistic ability to lie at the drop of a hat, but by the time of book five he has come to value her knack for nosing out situations and figuring out human nature. They work more in a symbiotic relationship now when she manages with good reason to insinuate herself into one of his cases. While he shows concern for her safety, he nevertheless respects her intuition.

One last point on voice. Over the years of writing Nora, I've been fortunate to have developed good friends in the UK who will answer stray questions when I'm doing research, but more importantly, form part of my beta readers to correct my "Britspeak," since Nora is the only American voice. I learned early on that much of the slang I used in first drafts came from older *Masterpiece Mysteries* and wasn't in vogue now. Those are the kinds of things that make having a personal contact in the area of your book's setting invaluable.

It's far easier in the Trudy series for my natural Yankee dialect to take over and I can clearly hear her voice. Despite living in North Carolina for the past 26 years, I haven't picked up much of a southern twang, and anyone hearing me speak can tell I'm a northerner. Just ask me to say "coffee."

Cozy Crime
in a Surveillance Society

M.E. Hilliard

Look up and count the cameras. As you go through an average day—work commute, school pick-up, errands—look around and note how many different types of surveillance you see. Then ask yourself, "How can I possibly commit murder in the middle of all of this?"

Getting away with murder, or any major crime, is difficult when electronic eyeballs seem to be everywhere. It's the contemporary cozy conundrum—creating a believable setting in which a crime can be committed without being caught on camera and then solved by an amateur sleuth who doesn't have access to all the same means of surveillance available to law enforcement. Readers will suspend disbelief to a point, but they're not going to buy an entire town with no doorbell cameras or CCTV and consistently unreliable cell phone service. How, then, to pull it off? Do you need to limit yourself to periods and places in which technology is not yet ubiquitous? Or is it possible to create a contemporary setting that allows for the successful perpetration and solving of a crime in spite of, or perhaps because of, the judicious use of current technology?

It *is* possible, and it presents opportunities for the kind of puzzle solving beloved of mystery readers—and writers. I read cozies because I'm more interested in the use of "little gray cells" than I am in forensics or high-tech surveillance. I like stories about average people doing in other average people with random items found around the home or office and then being brought to justice by a sleuth who uses their knowledge of human nature combined with a series of clues, shared with me, that lead to a logical conclusion. No blood, no gore, no crime scene unit, no computer hackers—just plain old deduction with a detective and setting I enjoy. I write cozies for the same reasons.

Why contemporary? Why not stick with a time period where

technology doesn't render old-fashioned detecting obsolete? Because, like most of you, I know in my heart that I am a great detective! For me, it's all about solving the puzzle, and as a writer, I get to create the puzzle as well. When choosing a setting, I factor in what skills both my detective and my murderer will need when dealing with the technology they're likely to find there and what resources will be available to them. This requires a combination of research and creative problem solving.

Before we choose a setting, let's review what constitutes surveillance in today's highly wired society. Gone are the days when tracking a suspect's movements required a stake-out and time spent following them around. Gone is a world where the only places you'd find security cameras are businesses and the homes of the wealthy. It's not only the bad guys who have to think about these things. Your detective is going to have a harder time snooping around without anyone noticing. Once upon a time, Sue Grafton's Kinsey Millhone could lurk outside a suspect's home, clock their exit time, and discreetly nose through their trash and maybe even their mail, her only concern the nosy neighbor. Now she'd have to contend with all of the above and doorbell cameras as well.

In addition to an increase in security cameras, CCTV, doorbell cameras, traffic cameras, and motion detectors attached to outdoor lights, both your murderer and your detective now have to contend with the kind of incidental surveillance brought about by other people's cell phone cameras and social media. It's easy to get caught in the background of someone's video or picture while attending an event or just going about your business. Depending on your own social media use and settings, you can also be tagged in someone else's post. That's an alibi confirmed or blown. If your suspect has a day job in a building with more modern security or is staying in a modern chain hotel, she's going to be logged in and out every time she uses her badge or key card.

Seems insurmountable, doesn't it? It isn't, really, but it does require some research on your part to verify the amount and type of surveillance and technology available in your chosen setting. You then need to do regular plausibility checks as you plot to see if whatever you're using is appropriate in terms of geography, weather, finances, and demographics. So where to begin?

Traditional cozy mystery settings offer a great starting point. After all, even the Golden Age authors had to contend with telephones, telegrams, and the proximity of Scotland Yard with all its resources. These settings have the advantage of coming with some built-in expectations on the part of the reader—the country house will have iffy communications in and out, and the village gossips will spot a sketchy newcomer faster than the local cops. You can use them as is, updating the types of technology that fail and when, or take the basic idea of the location and add a twist.

For example, update the traditional cut telephone wires, cryptic scribbles on the desk blotter, and compromising photos with a cell phone dead zone, internet browser history, and a clue in the background of someone's selfie, and you've got a nice evidence trail. The key is choosing a setting that offers both your criminal and your detective access to a plausible amount and type of technology suitable to the location. Start with something feasible, and you can create additional limitations and opportunities using character and plot without losing your readers.

Let's take a look at some of the more common settings and evaluate our options, then consider some contemporary spins.

The country house:

In the hundred-plus years since Agatha Christie published *The Mysterious Affair at Styles*, the country house murder has become a mystery mainstay. As a cozy setting, it has a lot to recommend it. By its nature, the country house is some distance from the nearest big city and on the outskirts of the nearest town. The bucolic setting lends itself to country roads that aren't littered with traffic cameras, cell and internet service that are not always reliable, and neighbors whose doorbell cameras are unlikely to offer a view all the way down their winding driveways. You can play this straight and have your circle of suspects summoned by Great Uncle Moneybags, an eccentric billionaire who demands that all devices be turned over to Evans, his majordomo, who will lock them in a safe which only Moneybags can open. Possible? Yes. Believable? Given what we see in the news about eccentric billionaires and what the average person is willing to do for money—also, yes. Besides, it saves you the trouble of having to come up with a plot point that knocks out the nearest cell tower. But if you'd rather, you can always manufacture a nor'easter or a blizzard that will not only kill communications but will also render the roads impassable. Throw in a power outage and let the games begin!

This scenario plays it straight with the classic country house mystery—your detective has to rely on her wits and physical evidence. To give it a more contemporary spin, add some technology back. Perhaps Great Uncle Moneybags was secretly surveilling his guests for nefarious reasons of his own. Or perhaps Evans was, and a guest does in one or both because of it and is erasing the evidence when the power goes out. Never underestimate the value of bad weather to undermine a surveillance system of any kind, electronic or human. So now you have a bit of evidence—at least until the battery backup runs down. Connie Berry does a nice job of this kind of update in *A Dream of Death* set in the Scottish Hebrides at an old family home, complete with caretaker cottages. Berry uses the remote location, unpredictable weather, and a somewhat updated but not state-of-the art security system to provide a believable amount of technology.

A useful subset of the country house setting is the vacation home on an island. The best known of these is Christie's *And Then There Were None*. Jane Haddam updated it in the nineties with *And One to Die On*. Neither author had to contend with the current prevalence of cell phones, but both had to factor in curious townspeople on land and the combination of flashlights and Morse code. They handled it differently but effectively. A more current take on this is Tessa Wegert's *Death in the Family*, which takes place in the Thousand Islands region of upstate New York. Wegert uses the location and seasonal bad weather to allow for intermittent connectivity and no immediate hope of help coming by boat, and the setting makes this entirely plausible. With privacy an increasingly hard to come by luxury, an island retreat with controlled physical and electronic access would hold great appeal for a range of people, from old money to newly minted movie star. That gives you a lot to work with.

If you don't want to stick with the old family manor trope, there are plenty of ways to repurpose the country house setting to bring it up to date. Perhaps now it's a traditional bed and breakfast or a boutique hotel. It could also be a spa or a corporate retreat center. All of these options maintain the rural location and allow for situations in which technology of any sort can be limited but not eliminated. The B&B is offering a *Bridgerton*-themed weekend—no devices allowed. The spa wants you to unplug, so hand over that cell phone. The corporate retreat center is all about team-building exercises, so leave your laptops at home. All of these are likely to have some kind of surveillance system in place, but depending on desired ambiance and funding, the new owners of the family estate are likely to stick with the old-school lock and key method, rather than key card access, and what cameras there are will be limited to public areas. Whatever system is in place, you have the option of having a character disable it or work around it. You'll also have characters that break the rules, because that's human nature. That can be your murderer, a valuable witness (once you get them to 'fess up to illicit laptop use) or even your detective. What matters is that the parameters you create are consistent and feasible for the setting.

Another traditional cozy setting that can be effectively updated is the village or small town. Though we've come a long way from St. Mary Mead or even Cabot Cove, the village is still a viable setting. G.M. Malliet uses it very effectively in her Max Tudor Mysteries, a contemporary series set in the fictional village of Nether Monkslip. The village setting shares several advantages with the country house. Locating it anywhere from just off the beaten path to a far-flung location, you have the possibility of spotty cell service, interrupted internet, and weather-related power outages. Consider too the fact that not every intersection is going to have a traffic camera—there are always low usage roads that don't merit them, and as any local will tell you, you can always go the back way. If your murderer is not particular about the type of transportation, you've also got dirt roads, bridle paths, and bike trails. Funding for surveillance equipment and monitoring is also a crapshoot—the more rural the area, the less likely it is that the law enforcement budget will stretch to blanketing the area with cameras.

While the downtown area of your little village will have a certain number of businesses with CCTV and houses with doorbell cameras, it won't be consistent. Some won't have them, and of those that do, some won't use them. Ditto the outskirts of the community—even if you have critical mass of doorbell cameras, not all will be functioning at any given time. It only takes a few nights of being awakened at 3 a.m. by a marauding raccoon for potential witnesses to decide to mute their notifications and then to forget to check the system regularly or to decide to turn it off entirely. It's this very inconsistency that works in your favor as you plot. Catching one or more of your suspects on camera here or there can provide clues—or red herrings—but not conclusive evidence. Conversely, if your killer is familiar with which cameras are live and which aren't, she can make appearances designed to misdirect. Bring the village grapevine back into play by having her odd perambulations witnessed by one of the local gossips.

As far as internet access goes, you obviously can't cut it off to the whole town. Even if your detective can't access it from where they are, there's always the free Wi-Fi at the local public library or coffee shop. This is where you have to keep in mind that not all public records are online, not all social media pages are public, and a suspect's web presence may have been curated to produce a desired effect. Once again, you have the opportunity to parcel out information. However, while you will find social media influencers everywhere, which public records are available online will vary by jurisdiction. A string of traffic tickets—yes. A probated will— no. You'll need to do your research when choosing your setting and see if that real estate transaction from 1972 that will provide a vital clue has been digitized or if your sleuth will need to take a trip to the county clerk's office to look it up.

A popular variation on the village setting is the boarding school or college. This gets tricky, because now you're dealing with a group of people who learned from an early age to scrub their social media pages of anything that would reflect badly on them in order to gain entrée to the school of their choice. If you're not in this cohort or working with them, you'll really need to do your homework. On the upside, if most of your suspects are presenting an incomplete or false persona to the world, your detective will have to rely less on technology and more on old school skills like gossiping and snooping around. Of course, murder in the faculty lounge is just as likely as murder among the students and gives you a variety of demographics to work with, from the tech-savvy recent hire to the tenured Luddite. Your setting is the academic community that constitutes the school—the physical campus can be placed anywhere that suits your story and allows for the kind of surveillance and connectivity, or lack thereof, that works with your plot.

All of these settings lean on traditional tropes for choice of setting, but you can place your story anywhere you can find a closed circle of suspects and an amount of technology that's reasonable for the location. I choose settings that I either know or will enjoy researching. The community theater that can't afford a security system, the auction house with the metal roof that kills cell phone signals, the co-op building whose residents steadfastly refuse any updates that will impinge upon their privacy—everything is fair game. As you go about your life, from weekend errands to school field trips to vacation, take note of what kind of surveillance is in use and how everyday technology functions or doesn't. Wherever you are, figure out how you would commit a crime there and what options an amateur would have for solving it. In other words, case the joint. What kind of key do you need to get in? Is there a security guard? How's your cell phone signal? Wi-Fi? Are there lots of people taking selfies? Can you find a map or floor plan online? And, of course, look up and count the cameras.

PART FOUR

Writing Character

What Makes a Cozy Character

Amanda Flower

In the world of mystery, the cozy subgenre is known for no graphic sex or violence, very little foul language, if any, and host of supporting characters, the quirkier the better. Another interesting aspect of the subgenre is the focus on the main character above focus on plot. Most mystery novels are plot driven, and in some, like standalone thrillers, the reader knows very little about the protagonist's personal life. That is not the case in a cozy mystery. Readers truly get to know a cozy protagonist and may even know her better than some of their own friends and family. This is especially the case over a long-running series, where the author has the opportunity to dig into every little detail that makes the main character tick and encompasses her life.

But what makes a great cozy protagonist? What are the characteristics that most cozy main characters share? Are there rules? Can the rules be broken and a book still be considered a cozy? And why do they all have goofy pets? I hope to answer those questions.

I have written nearly fifty cozy mysteries across my writing career and have had a wide variety of cozy protagonists from a keeper of a magical garden to an elderly Amish widow. Mystery is my favorite genre, and cozy is my favorite subgenre. I also write historical mystery, which I love, buy my heart belongs to cozy.

After writing so many cozies over nine series, it can be a challenge to make my protagonists different from each other. I do that with giving them different life experiences, different backgrounds, and different personalities. Aside from the personal characteristics about the protagonist, the setting and time period of the story also contribute to make one character different from another. Where and when a person is in the world can be very telling in who they are. Making my characters different is something that I have to be constantly vigilant about as I would not want a reader to pick up one series and say, "This is just like her other series."

As conscious as I am about their differences for the sake of this essay, I will concentrate on their similarities. What are those things *most*, not all, cozy protagonists have in common? I have come up with eleven key characteristics, all of which I will explain, and then I will discuss if those rules can be bent or even broken.

The first and most important characteristic that every cozy protagonist needs is curiosity. A detective of any type has to want to know the truth. This is especially true for a cozy sleuth because a cozy sleuth really has no business solving a crime. She must have an innate desire to know why the crime was committed. If she does not, then she would gladly leave it up to the proper authorities to solve the crime. Many times, this curiosity is sparked with some connection with the murder. The sleuth is a suspect herself, knows a suspect, or knows the victim. This is her connection to poking her nose where it doesn't belong.

Along with an innate curiosity, a cozy sleuth must have a clear understanding of what she believes is right and wrong. She must want to see justice served. She doesn't want the investigation to be wrapped up quickly if that means the wrong person is accused of the crime, and she will relentlessly stay on the case until the right culprit is discovered and held accountable.

Another characteristic of a cozy protagonist is occupation other than law enforcement. As a general rule a cozy sleuth doesn't have a reason to investigate a crime because of their occupation. They can be just about anything else. Shopkeeper, librarian, and crafter are some of the most popular occupations. I've used them all myself, and many times, the protagonist's occupation helps solve the crime because she noticed some detail others, such as the police, can miss.

No matter what the protagonist's occupation is, the main character has to be smart. How else could she be able to solve the crime when the police are left baffled? Her intelligence is demonstrated in asking the right questions of suspects, making clear observations, and being willing to question those in authority when she feels like something is off. Many times in cozy, there is something that the sleuth understands or knows, which can be anything from how a contraption works or the personality of one the suspects, that allows her to come to a logical conclusion.

Along with intelligence, a cozy protagonist must have emotional intelligence and that includes compassion. A cozy sleuth becomes involved in a crime because she cares. She cares for the victim, one of the suspects, or someone who is deeply impacted by the crime, such as a relative of the victim. As a cozy series goes on and on over many books, it can be a challenge for the author to connect the main character to the person she has compassion for in a believable way. What helps with that is having a large cast of supporting characters, all of whom can be tangled up in a criminal investigation at one point.

Compassion is essential but so is hard work. Cozy sleuths are some of the hardest working characters in fiction. Not only do they have to run a shop, knit, manage a library, or own a hair salon, they have to solve a murder. Many times they are juggling both of these things because the character needs to have a "real job" while solving the crime. In order to be running off and investigating all the time, in many of these cases the main character depends on her family and friends to hold down the fort when it pertains to her job or business while she is solving the crime. She may be in and out of the shop, but she needs another character at her place of work all the time in order to keep the business open. For this reason a good supporting cast for the sleuth is key.

Cozy sleuths are also known for having a quirky supporting cast. In a cozy, readers not only get to know the protagonist and the victim and suspects involved in the crime but they also get to know the sleuth's family and friends, who may or may not be involved in the investigation. These characters are added to give the sleuth more grounding for the reader, so that the reader will want to come back to the series again and again. One of the goals of the cozy is to make the reader think of the protagonist as a friend.

In addition to a quirky supporting cast, most cozy sleuths have an equally quirky animal sidekick. Now, this one is not true in all cozies, but I think it is safe to say it is extremely common. Many times, it is the animal sidekick who makes the covers of these novels. Like human friends and family, the animal sidekicks are added to the plots in order to make the main characters more relatable because everyone has experience chasing a dog that got out or being ignored by a cat. These slice of life details make the character more normal even though she is doing extraordinary things, mainly solving a murder. Also in many cases, they are added for comic relief.

Comic relief is an important element in a cozy, and that's why a cozy sleuth needs to have a good sense of humor. Many cozies are written in first person, which is another tactic authors use to make readers believe that they have a friendship with the character. The main character's personality, humor, and wit can easily be interwoven into the prose. Sense of humor is the likely the most important of these because many readers love cozies because it is a form of escapism. It gives them a chance to leave their everyday lives and enjoy a good story. Adding humor to the story with amusing dialogue or zany side characters can break the tension in the novel, allowing readers to take a breath and enjoy the story. If the readers chuckle along the way, it is all the better.

Along with a quirky animal character, it helps if the main character has a love interest. Typically, this individual is introduced in the first novel of the series, and the relationship can be a very slow burn over many books. This detail is included in cozy mysteries since readers want to see the main character as a real person and part of being a real person is having relationship issues. Many times, the love interests in these novels work for law enforcement, which not only gives the main character someone to care about but also gives her an in into the inner workings of law enforcement. At times, the love interest shares police information with the sleuth as their relationship grows and trust is built between the two. However, most of the time, this element adds an extra layer of tension to the story as the law enforcement love interest does not want the main character "muddling" in the case. This can cause the main character to have to choose between her romantic feelings and what she believes is right. Going back to that clear sense of right and wrong that cozy protagonists need, most of the time the cozy sleuth will choose what she believes is right over love. The best cases for the character are those situations in which she can have both. That tends to happen later in a series when the main character and love interest are committed to each other for the long run.

Finally, a cozy character has to be brave even if she doesn't believe that she is brave. Like all sleuths, cozy protagonists are faced with some very scary situations. At one point, they come face to face with the culprit and are in great danger. However, they also have to be brave enough to investigate a crime which they really have no business doing so. They have to be brave enough to question the police and those in authority in order to come to the right conclusion in the end. By doing this, they put their personal safety, livelihoods, and even at times their loved ones at great risk. Anyone who is willing to do that has to be brave.

These rules are more guidelines than rules. These are the standard characteristics that readers expect to see when reading a cozy. They don't always appear in a novel. For example, sometimes a novel is considered a cozy because it has humorous tone but the main character is a police officer. In that case the novel would technically be a crossover of a police procedural and cozy mystery. Other times, a novel is considered a cozy and the main character is on a trip alone and doesn't know any of the supporting cast. She doesn't have a connection with any of the characters other than being in the same place with them. This can be especially true in locked room or destination mysteries where the main character is out of her natural environment.

The bottom line is this list of characteristics is a guide, not a law book. Its goal is to better understand why readers see the same characteristics over and over again in a cozy mystery. They are tropes, and all fiction genres have tropes. Tropes can be used successfully or ignored completely by authors, but it's important that the authors in each genre understand what their audience is expecting so that they can write the most satisfying book for their readers.

Good writers know the rules and how to use them as well as how to bend and break them to their own will. They know even within the parameters of their genre how to make their main character unique, different, and appealing to their readers. In my case, after writing so many cozy mysteries with young protagonists who are returning home after being away in some sort of professional capacity, I wanted to do something completely different, so I started writing the *Amish Matchmaker Mysteries* for Kensington. My main character for this series is different from any other protagonist I have written. She is a sixty-eight-year-old Amish widow. She has generational, cultural, and life experiences that are different from any other character I write. Although more mature sleuths are becoming a bit more common, they are still unusual in the genre.

Ultimately, cozy sleuths are so popular and likable because readers can see themselves in that person's life. They relate to the main character. They care about her, and they want to see her succeed. And because they have a relationship with her, they are willing to come back again and again to the same series in order to see where that cozy sleuth is in her life and what kind of mess she got tangled up in this time. All the while, the reader is rooting for the sleuth, which was the author's hope and intention all along.

…And a Colorful Cast

Building a Diverse Cozy

KATHLEEN MARPLE KALB
(NIKKI KNIGHT)

We live in a world.

That's what I like to say when people ask me why I write mysteries set in the whitest state in the union with a Jewish main character, a Black police chief, several happily married gay couples, and a woman priest as part of the, yes, colorful cast of locals. People who don't read cozies tend to think of them as being written by, about, and for cute little white grandmothers. Anybody who's actually been reading cozies in recent years would take issue with that, of course, but the perception is there. In fact, much of the best work in the lighter end of the mystery spectrum these days is being done by writers of color and LGBTQ+ authors, who use their own life experiences as the basis for good cozy fun. Start with Mia Manasala, Jennifer J. Chow, and Rob Osler, and go from there.

But there's no reason clueless white chicks—guilty as charged!—can't, and shouldn't, do their bit to create cozies that are more reflective of the world today. Maybe it's even more our job, since we're benefiting from the very privilege that leads some people to pick up our books, so we have a chance to reach an audience who wouldn't necessarily try a more modern cozy.

By the time I started writing mysteries, diversity was a natural part of my world, but I sure didn't grow up that way. In my corner of Western Pennsylvania, we had one out gay couple and one Black family. It wasn't until college, where I had the benefit of a Black roommate and classmates of every color and sexual orientation, that I really got to know people who were different than me.

And love them.

The next couple of decades in newsrooms, and particularly working in a New York newsroom, just solidified what I'd learned: that everyone brings something different, and we are a much better world for all those perspectives. Admitting right up front that you don't know about someone else's life, but are willing to listen and understand, and it's your job to learn, not theirs to teach, is a great place to start.

None of that's easy work for anyone, and I was lucky enough to do it early and have it in my background when I started writing the Vermont Radio Mysteries. There was no question that my experience as a country girl who worked her way up to New York City, married a Jewish guy from the Bronx, and accidentally found a faith that spoke to her was going to inform the main character, Jaye Jordan. Since I write in first person, a lot of my perspective became hers, though she's more religiously observant, funnier, and a good bit more reckless than I am.

The people around Jaye borrowed from my experience too. Of course, she'd have some wonderful, un-dramatically gay friends who were happily married, like couples I've known over the years. Her girlfriends would be like mine: bringing a variety of backgrounds and perspectives, united by place and goals. One friend, who's Black, Alicia Orr, would borrow from one of my most beloved and admired colleagues, who grew up with the same emphasis on manners and demeanor as I did, creating a bond despite our wide gulf in lived experience.

It's still a story set in Vermont, though. The state is one of the most accepting for LGBTQ+ people in the nation, so the idea of married same-sex couples was no big deal. Figuring out how to make a racially diverse cast realistic was a bit more of a challenge.

When I started thinking about it, though, it wasn't really that hard at all.

A lot of highly professional New Yorkers move to Vermont to retire or for a simpler life. Why, then, couldn't an NYPD lieutenant let himself be recruited for the police chief job in tiny Simpson? And so was born Police Chief George Orr.

In the book and short stories, there are several references to town officials recruiting Chief George for the job, and to how he, his wife Alicia, and the town have adjusted to each other. It's clear that while they're happy, it isn't always easy. We often see the Chief or Alicia visiting Jaye at the station to talk about the current case and also enjoying a little uncomplicated time with a fellow New York transplant.

The goal was simple: to make my little fictional world look a bit more like our world in general, without forcing it into the story. The whole point, for me, is that we *do* live in that diverse world, so the characters are simply being who they are.

About that. As far as possible, I try to write characters like real people I know. Not in the sense of picking up a colleague and dropping them into the story, but in the sense of knowing someone well enough to create a character with a similar worldview and experience.

Alicia Orr, for example, borrows considerably from a woman I've worked with for nearly twenty years. She's Black, and grew up in a middle-class family of Caribbean descent in New York City. We bonded early on when we discovered that we were both raised with a strict code of ladylike manners: entirely different backgrounds, same emphasis on "knowing how to behave." That early understanding and long-growing friendship is similar to the dynamic between Alicia and Jaye.

An important note here, though, about cultural appropriation.

My "borrowing" from my colleagues and friends is in the service of creating a more diverse cast in a story that is told from the perspective of a cis, straight white woman. (Or, as I describe myself, a clueless white chick.) It involves a lot of listening and the occasional uncomfortable discussion, sometimes just the things that come up in daily relationships—and sometimes actively vetting plot points or character development.

Since I'm lucky enough to have a wide circle of friends and colleagues from all kinds of backgrounds and experiences, I'll discuss ideas with them. Often, too, I just listen and absorb the way they see things to make sure I have a good sense of their perspective.

While I'm doing the work every day to make sure that my cast is diverse, I'd never presume, for example, to write from the perspective of a person of color or an LGBTQ+ character. To me, that feels like appropriation, not creation.

There are some writers who can, and do, take on the perspective of a marginalized person and do a brilliant job of bringing their experience to light. That's their business, and I'll leave the debate over that to someone else. It's not for me.

In the context of a cozy, what's important is the idea that diversity is a good fit, and honestly it's not too hard to do. Cozies are known for a wide variety of quirky characters, after all. Why not take that idea and expand it to include the whole rainbow of human experience? Because, you see, that's the most important thing I've learned about diversity in my long career of working with folks from every imaginable background, orientation, and experience: it's fun.

When you're open to all kinds of different ideas and experiences, you can't help learning a lot, and one of the things you learn is that there are many enjoyable things you didn't know about in your little silo. It's fun for writers, and fun for readers, to bring in new kinds of people. Spending time in Tita Rosie's kitchen (Mia Manasala) or following a mystery through the Seattle gay scene (Rob Osler) is really just a wonderful new twist on the whole idea of cozy mysteries as escape.

Still, everybody isn't going to be on board with this.

When *Live, Local, and Dead*, the first Vermont Radio Mystery, was published, I kept getting a lot of complaints about the main character working too much with the police chief. "Why does she take evidence to him instead of solving it herself?" was a common thread. It wasn't until the third or fourth comment that I realized what the problem was. After all, cozy sleuths often work with—and sometimes date—the real cops. The problem was this particular cop, a six-foot-three Black man in an Indiana Jones fedora and leather trench coat who shares a respectful professional relationship with the main character. These readers were self-aware enough to know they don't want to be racist but not enough to realize that race is the reason they have a problem with Chief George. Nothing I can do about that, I decided. People will think what they like, and I can't change it. I won't.

It's a good example, though, of the flip side of expanding the cast. There are always going to be people who don't like what you're doing. But if you know it's right, you keep doing it, and eventually they'll catch on. Or they won't, and you'll still know you're doing the right thing.

Which I did. My most recent project (*The Stuff of Murder*, published in fall 2023 from Level Best Books) is led by a main character who's in the process of converting to Judaism, surrounded by a racially and ethnically diverse ensemble. Not to mention "the dads she should have had," and her young son, who has both a photographic memory and Type-1 Diabetes.

Somebody's probably not going to like it.

But we live in a world.

I'm Okay, Really

Writing a Main Character Who Has an Addiction or a Mental Health Disorder

J.C. KENNEY

I've been a mystery fan all my life. This love affair began as a pre-schooler with those meddling kids from *Scooby-Doo*. It grew into novels when I was introduced to Agatha Christie as a teenager. Since then, I've read, watched, and listened to mysteries of all kinds—thrillers, police procedurals, private eye novels, romantic suspense, gothic horror mysteries.

One of the hills I'm even willing to die on is my belief that *Leviathan Wakes*, Book One in James S.A. Corey's immensely popular *The Expanse* series, is a police procedural at heart. It just happens to be set in outer space. There's little doubt that if a story involves a mystery, count me in.

Of all the genres within the wonderful world of mystery fiction, though, my favorite is the cozy.

From my perspective, both as a writer and as a reader, the allure of the cozy mystery is straightforward. As a puzzle is unraveled, wrongs are righted, evildoers are brought to justice, and order is restored to the community. In short, the good guys come out on top. Hooray for our intrepid protagonist, who, despite the odds, manages to take down the villain using their wits, some dogged determination, and the support of a close friend or two.

Our cozy mystery protagonists don't have unearthly powers like super hearing. That would come in handy when eavesdropping on a murder suspect. They don't have access to game- changing technology like facial recognition software, either. How handy would that be when trying to figure out the identity of the shadowy figure photographed fleeing the scene of the crime? They're not even members of law enforcement, so they don't have access to things like police radios and arrest powers.

No, in the world of cozy mysteries, the protagonist is just like us. An average, run of the mill soul with bills to pay and family to worry about. They have jobs, good friends, and cute pets. On the whole, they're pretty well-adjusted folks.

Well, most of them are. Here are a few examples of well-known characters who aren't quite so well adjusted.

Agatha Raisin, the namesake of the long-running cozy series from M.C. Beaton, isn't the most pleasant soul to hang around with. Given the neglect and abuse she suffered at the hands of her parents when she was growing up and then her husband, it's no wonder she's standoffish and is lacking in the friend department. Temperance Brennan, the lead character in the hit show *Bones*, carries the emotional weight of her parents' disappearance with her every day. Those scars have left her distrustful of others, which is evident in her "prickly" personality. The beloved Adrian Monk struggles mightily with depression and anxiety in the aftermath of his wife's murder. When we go all the way back to the nineteenth century, we find Sherlock Holmes investigating crime while living with an opium addiction.

The protagonists in my mysteries, Allie Cobb and Darcy Gaughan, have their mental health challenges too. Allie lives with anxiety that stems from being bullied by other kids as a child. In addition to that, after the death of her father in *A Literal Mess*, book one of the Allie Cobb Mysteries, she begins to develop symptoms of depression.

Darcy lost her career as the leader of a punk rock band in large part due to her abuse of alcohol. When we meet her in *Record Store Reckoning*, Book One of the Darcy Gaughan Mysteries, she's been sober for five years, but the challenges she faces due to her addiction are always close at hand.

Mental health conditions like anxiety and depression are heavy issues. So why add them to stories that already involve murder? After all, cozy mysteries already feature more "positive" aspects like an intriguing puzzle, a community full of characters the reader wants to get to know, and a satisfying resolution to the crime. It's like my mom told me why she read Agatha Christie. "It's about the puzzle, not about the murder."

While all of that is true, I think there's value in writing characters, especially the protagonist, who live with the same problems and health conditions many readers live with every day.

In recent years, we've heard the phrase "Representation matters" more and more often. This applies to life in the workplace, right along with popular music and literature. People from all walks of life want to see, listen to, and read about characters who are like them. Including cozy mysteries. When we read about characters who are like us, we're able to connect with a community. We feel less alone. It doesn't matter that the cozy mystery is a work of fiction. What matters is that we feel seen.

When we accept the premise that readers want to experience characters like themselves, and we should, a question comes up. How many people are we talking about? When it comes to folks with a mental health condition, the numbers are staggering. According to the Johns Hopkins School of Medicine, about one in every four Americans over the age of eighteen suffers from a diagnosable mental health disorder every year. That amounts to literally tens of millions of people in the United States alone.

Here's another hard truth. The majority of people who commit suicide have a diagnosable mental health condition. Most often those conditions are a depressive order or a substance abuse disorder. Living with a mental health disorder is hard. Even when the condition has been diagnosed and the person living with it is receiving appropriate medical care.

I know.

I spent the summer of 2011 plotting how to take my own life. A plan was in place. All that remained was to decide on a date. Fortunately, I didn't follow through. Instead, I confided in my wife. It was one of the toughest confessions I've ever made. After that, I sought help and was diagnosed with clinical depression in February 2012.

As the saying goes, I'm feeling much better now. Even on medication, though, I have my good days and my bad days. The bad days can be exhausting, both mentally and physically.

The thing is, for people with a mental health disorder, the condition isn't visible to the naked eye. There are no indicators like a cast on a broken bone or a scar from surgery to remove a cancerous tumor. Because of that lack of obvious physical signs, over the years, living with a mental health disorder became stigmatized and led to accusations like the ones below.

You're too exhausted to get out of bed? You're lazy, not depressed.

You crave alcohol? It's due to some sort of a moral failing or weakness, not a chemical dependence.

Neither of those are true. There are countless chronic medical conditions that don't carry a stigma with them. Arthritis, high cholesterol, elevated blood pressure, osteoporosis. Those health conditions, and so many more, don't carry the negative connotation that mental health disorders do. Science tells us that mental health conditions are the result of genetic factors as much as environmental ones. Someone's brain may be wired differently from the day they were born. Someone else may develop a mental health condition because of something that happened in their life. Either way, just because their mind works differently than normal shouldn't mean that person should be looked down upon.

That's why efforts to erase that stigma are so important. One way to do that is to have open and honest conversations about mental health.

Robin Williams, God bless his soul, helped so many people when he talked about his mental health and the challenges he faced every day. Readers have contacted me to express their thanks for the compassionate yet honest way I address mental health in my books.

That's one of the benefits of being an author. The opportunity to connect with people in a meaningful way.

Now that I've talked a bit about the why, I'd like to turn to how I present these issues in my books. Nobody wants to spend their precious leisure hours being beaten over the head about a heavy issue like mental health, after all. I don't know about you, but I'm inundated by commercials for the latest wonder drug when I'm watching television. Books can be an escape from that, so I work mental health issues into the stories in an organic way.

My protagonists may live with mental health conditions. They aren't defined by them, though. When you think of Holmes and Monk, what comes to mind? Their brilliant investigatory skills. Agatha Raisin? Her unwillingness to give up. Temperance Brennan? Her determination to find answers for the families of the murder victims that come across her exam table.

The same goes for my amateur sleuths. Allie Cobb's a successful literary agent. Some folks in her hometown of Rushing Creek, Indiana, think she's pushy and don't care for her investigatory tactics. She doesn't let the opinions of others, or her anxiety, stop her search for the truth, though.

Darcy Gaughan runs an independent record store that's a keystone for her community. She doesn't shy away from the fact that she hurt a lot of people, including herself, when her alcohol abuse was at its worst. She's accepted responsibility for her past decisions. While some in town hold her past behavior against her, she uses the fact that others helped her when she was at her lowest point as motivation to help others.

I'm not suggesting that Allie and Darcy are bulletproof. Investigating murder, even in a cozy mystery, can take a toll on a person. This is where I believe it is important to weave some, but not too much, reality into the story. The amateur sleuth in a cozy mystery isn't a professional in law enforcement with training on how to cope with the ugliness of the criminal world.

For Allie, this toll manifests itself in recurring insomnia and nightmares when she can get to sleep. Initially, alternative treatments like aromatherapy and meditation help her cope. By the time she's investigated her third murder, she comes to accept the fact that she needs help from a professional therapist to help her deal with the trauma she's come face to face with.

In real life, people seek help from counselors and therapists every day. That's okay. The effect trauma has on us is real. It can be acute, like from discovering a dead body. It can be the result of something chronic, like anxiety from being bullied year after year while growing up.

The situation is different with Darcy. Her alcohol abuse disorder left her literally in the gutter long before she began solving murders. With help from close friends, she entered a treatment facility. While there, she got sober and learned techniques to help her respond to stressful situations in ways that weren't harmful to herself or others. Those anxiety-management skills, like taking slow, deep breaths and visualizing calming scenes, come in handy when she's on a case. She's learned to recognize the warning signs, so when she's hit with a panic attack, she knows how to respond.

Living with a mental health disorder isn't easy. But folks all over the world do it every day. They go to work, fall in love, get married, take vacations, and read cozy mysteries.

I believe there's great value in showing characters with mental health conditions like anxiety, depression, and alcohol use disorder in cozy mysteries. Not every amateur sleuth will be as well-adjusted as Jane Marple. Authors are given unique opportunities to build inclusive worlds in our little cozy communities. When one in every eight people around the world lives with a mental health disorder, we'd be remiss not to include characters with those same health conditions in our mysteries. It's my hope that by including characters like that in my books, I can help build empathy for those who live with them in real life. At the same time, I'm also trying to do my part to erase the stigma around mental health.

Cozy mysteries are stories where there's a lot more to the amateur sleuth than meets the eye. We don't dismiss them because of their age, gender, or family background. Nor should we dismiss them if their brain is wired differently than normal. In real life, we should strive for everyone in society to have the opportunity to contribute. Let's do the same in cozy mysteries.

Writing a Highly Sensitive Amateur Sleuth

Carol E. Ayer

A cozy mystery protagonist is usually pretty perfect. She's friendly and a go-getter, confident and energetic. She balances her work, relationships, and murder investigations with ease. If she does have a "negative" quality, it's something cute and fun—like a sweet tooth, a tendency to babble, or the propensity to land herself in humorous situations, all things readers enjoy hearing about. Although there may be a growing trend toward more realistic heroines in cozies, ones who struggle with alcoholism, widowhood, or mental illness, the perky and flawless cozy protagonist reigns supreme.

After all, cozies, which typically blend sweet romance with mystery, are fundamentally designed to be a means of escape, a lighthearted bit of entertainment. Readers want to go along for the ride of a murder investigation and perhaps finger the killer themselves, but they don't want to hear the gruesome details of the crime nor have the story veer off into the harsh realities of "real life."

I created Kayla Jeffries, my protagonist in the HSP Mysteries, partly because I had never read a work of fiction in which an HSP (Highly Sensitive Person) was featured. I myself am an HSP. As authors are often told to "write the book you want to read" and "write what you know," creating an HSP protagonist seemed like a good idea when I conceived of the series in late 2017. I could use my own experience to flesh out Kayla's character and hopefully educate readers about the HSP trait as well as tell an entertaining story.

The term "HSP" was first coined by Elaine Aron in the 1990s. Approximately one out of every five people (animals as well, which may explain why your cat dives under the bed at the slightest provocation) takes in more sensory data and processes it more deeply than a non–HSP. This often results in an unpleasant feeling of overstimulation and an over-whelming desire to escape the situation. To give a personal example, I recently had to leave my house when a neighbor had her trees trimmed. My heartrate had picked up uncomfortably and an unreasonable anger had surfaced in my chest. Non-HSPs may have been able to ignore the sound; for me, that wasn't a possibility: noise is a very big deal for Highly Sensitive People. An extra-sensitivity to strong smells and rough textures isn't uncommon, either. The titular character in the fairytale "The Princess and the Pea" was probably an HSP.

But it's not just their finely-attuned senses that can throw HSPs into a tailspin. HSPs tend to take on the emotions of those around them, in addition to regularly struggling with their own. To avoid absorbing everyone else's moods, they may prefer to be alone. HSPs are especially bothered by criticism and disagreements, and they need a long time to rebound from negative experiences.

All in all, the trait can make life difficult, as highly sensitives struggle to deal with the fast-paced, social media–fueled, chaotic world around them. Sure, everyone is stressed these days, but HSPs take it to another level.

Besides the fact that I myself identify as one, I had good reasons to make Kayla an HSP. HSPs are adept at reading other people and noticing details others miss, qualities any good detective possesses. At the same time, a built-in conflict presented itself. Kayla might be good at solving murders because of her acute attention to detail, her ability to tell when someone is lying, and her talent of coming up with creative solutions to the puzzle of a crime, but if there were a worse person to become involved in crime-fighting, it's an HSP. How overstimulating and overwhelming and stressful! But ... in fiction, conflict is good. Here I had a heroine who would, on the one hand, be good at solving crimes, but on the other, would naturally shy away from sleuthing to protect her sensitive nervous system. Surely a winning combination.

But it can't be denied that introverted and sensitive Kayla subverts the stereotype of a cozy mystery heroine. She doesn't share the bright-eyed, bushy-tailed personality that cozy protagonists are known for. With her easily-overwhelmed disposition, Kayla is anything but perky and energetic. Her concentration is swiftly broken by an irritating noise; a squabble with a friend crowds out all other thoughts; she tires quickly and needs lots of sleep.

Was it a risk to make my heroine a character who at first blush doesn't fit the cozy mold? I confess, perhaps naively, I didn't think it would be a problem. Sure, Kayla has a trait that can be problematic for her, but so what? I felt any qualities that might hinder her success would be balanced out by the strengths that she shares with other HSPs, which include compassion, creativity, and conscientiousness. The truth is, I *did* hold back when I created her, but not when it came to her HSP trait. If there's a scale of "HSP-ness," Kayla is at the extreme end, particularly bothered by loud noises (she hates doorbells and leaf blowers) and scratchy fabrics against her skin; she often doesn't like to be touched, even by someone she loves. No, I didn't pull any punches when it came to her highly sensitive trait. But HSPs often suffer from anxiety and depression—I do—and while Kayla can certainly feel down or nervous at times, she doesn't wrestle with those disorders. I thought I was keeping things "light" by not adding those struggles to her character profile.

I was rather alarmed, and admittedly a little put-out, when a colleague wrote to me in a direct message as we were both going through the submission process: "[Kayla] might give you some probs as apparently they [publishers] don't want them to be too flawed." But Kayla wasn't *flawed* ... was she? After all, being highly sensitive is just a trait, like having green eyes or freckles. But would publishers—and readers—consider Kayla flawed and not want to read about her adventures?

None of the editors who read my submission had a problem with my hook, at least not one they told my agent about. In addition to the standard "the setting didn't grab me" and "I wasn't drawn in," my rejections included lines such as "I loved the HSP angle" and "I enjoyed the new twist for a cozy series." Of course, these were still rejections, so who knows? In the end, I signed a contract for a three-book series with Camel Press in April of 2018, precisely because my editor, like me, had never seen an HSP featured as an amateur sleuth, and she thought it was a worthy hook.

Once I turned in *Peppermint Cream Die* in August 2018 (because this was my second traditionally-published novel, I only had to come up with a synopsis and three chapters when submitting), it was several months before I discussed the manuscript with my editor. By that time, problems with my protagonist had arisen. In a phone call she initiated, she stressed that I had to make Kayla likeable enough so that readers wouldn't hope they'd never meet an HSP in real life. *Ouch.* In her edit letter, she reiterated it was important to have a likeable character who faces difficulty but isn't overcome by it. *Huh.* That sounded like she *did* think Kayla's trait could be a problem.

Although I understood her point, it was important for me to convey what it's like to be an HSP, both on behalf of my HSP readers and those who had never heard of the trait. If one in five people is an HSP, that's a huge portion of the population begging to be known. Ideally, I'd help someone discover they were highly sensitive and that revelation would be life-changing, just as it had been for me when I first read Elaine Aron's seminal work *The Highly Sensitive Person*. But I also took the notes to heart. It became a balancing act, to make Kayla cheerful and appealing but to also show her very real struggles.

One thing I chose to do was begin the book *after* Kayla had learned about her trait and had adjusted her life accordingly. At the start of *Peppermint Cream Die*, she's living in a seaside town in a cottage close to the water—a place she loves. She's working as a home baker, a job she enjoys. She has a handle on how to cope with stress. Baking or a quick walk by the water calms her when she's overstimulated. She has a bestie, Isabella Valera, as well as other good friends, including soon-to-be murder victim 89-year-old Trudy Dillingham. Overall, she's in a good place.

It's only because she cares so much for Trudy that she dares get involved in the strain of a murder investigation. Early on in *Peppermint Cream Die*, she tells Isabella, "It sounds like a lot of stress. Way too much stress. But I can't sit back and hope the police find the person. I have to do something." Indeed, she does experience overstimulation while investigating and needs time to regroup, a departure from the typical "go, go, go" heroine who flits from her job to caring for her relationships to solving the crime.

The second book in the series, titled *Stabbed in the Tart*, sees Kayla as a suspect herself. When she starts losing business because she's being questioned for the murder of a fellow cook, she embarks on a quest to clear her name. In *Sourdough Dead*, the final book in the series, it's Kayla's boyfriend, Jason Banks, who finds himself in hot water when *he* becomes a suspect. In each installment, Kayla has a very good reason to become involved in the investigations. She would never *voluntarily* play amateur sleuth, say, to experience the "thrills" of a murder investigation—something the standard cozy heroine could legitimately be accused of.

In some ways, though, Kayla *is* a typical heroine. Like many a cozy protagonist, she adores her cats, despite being initially reluctant to adopt Trudy's orphaned feline, Sugar. She tells Isabella, "I can't take care of a pet. It's hard enough taking care of myself." Kayla has to weigh the pros and cons of owning a pet before she makes what she considers to be a huge life decision.

Even though Kayla works alone from the privacy of her own kitchen, she is a baker, a common profession for a cozy heroine. Also, like most amateur sleuths, Kayla has a best friend to bounce ideas off of. In true HSP fashion, sometimes she needs to process an experience solo before turning to her friend (as seen in *Stabbed in the Tart*, when she is faced for the second time with a dead body), but she and Isabella are still very close.

Cozy protagonists often have ups and downs in their love relationships and Kayla is no exception, but there are unique reasons behind her rocky love life. At the beginning of *Peppermint Cream Die*, she's recently broken up with a man who had become impatient with her sensitivity. It's taken a while for Kayla to get over this loss, and she isn't particularly looking for a new relationship. On the night of Trudy's murder, feeling out of sorts, she seeks out a comforting bowl of clam chowder. She meets Jason for the first time at the restaurant he owns and manages, and she gets her bowl of clam chowder as well as a potential new client and love interest. They begin dating soon afterward. They get along well, but a problem pops up by the end of the story. The very last line of *Peppermint Cream Die* is Jason professing his love for Kayla, a development she isn't ready for. *Stabbed in the Tart* deals with the fallout. By the end of that book, Kayla has confessed she loves him, too (she just needed time to realize it), and the two are back on track. It is only at the very end of the third book that another problem surfaces—Kayla doesn't sleep well when Jason stays over. This acknowledgment, plus an uncomfortable visit from her mother, brings her to question whether HSPs should live alone. She decides to risk it and agrees to Jason's marriage proposal, a typical cozy heroine reaction if there ever was one.

Like her cozy mystery cohorts, Kayla is a successful sleuth, mostly because of the advantages her trait confers. In Book 1, her attention to detail helps her rescue Isabella, who has been kidnapped by the killer. In Book 2, the unveiling of the murderer hinges on a case of mistaken identity that she alone realizes. Book 3 sees her putting together a couple of seemingly unrelated facts that lead her to the perpetrator.

On paper, then, Kayla doesn't diverge all that far from the cozy heroine norm. But are her minor differences preventing readers from embracing her? I don't think so. Although a couple of reviewers have complained that the books place too much emphasis on the HSP trait, most have liked Kayla and her sensitivity. Some of the comments have included "I enjoyed learning about HSP and what people with it deal with," "Kayla was an enjoyable heroine to get to know," and "I found her believable, enjoyable, [and] daring."

Sounds pretty perfect to me.

Why I Wrote a Buddy Cop Series with a Lesbian and a Jew

Winnie Frolik

Why did I decide to write a series of books with a lesbian heroine in 1930s Britain? The short answer is I didn't "decide" to do anything. I started writing a story and as it happened my main character Mary Grey happened to be gay. When she appeared on the page, it was much a surprise to me as to anyone else. Such is the mystery of writing.

The longer version is this: I have always been drawn to stories about society's outsiders. Particularly outsiders with secrets. I like to write such characters, and a dear friend (and editor) of mine once referred to it as my "trademark." When I decided to try writing a murder mystery this seemed like a perfect alignment. Detective stories by definition are about ferreting out the various secrets held by the entire cast of characters, aka suspects. My district nurse was always intended to be an investigator and truth seeker in the story. But that didn't mean she couldn't have a secret herself. Quite the contrary. It seemed particularly important that she did have one! But what would it be? Something to do with her private life, I reasoned. And thus it came to me that the seaside town Illhenny's beloved district nurse Mary Grey was hiding her sexuality. Once written it seemed inevitable.

This, in turn, added another wrinkle to the story, for in a sense Mary's secret was the most dangerous of all. (Yes, arguably even more so than murder.) Homosexuality among men in England at that time was illegal. Homosexuality among women hadn't been officially banned but only because the British Parliament feared putting such a law on the books would draw further attention to lesbians and entice more women to "experiment." Besides which it was assumed at the time that lesbianism was so rare among women it was almost statistically irrelevant. Natural born "spinster" types like Miss Marple did not arouse the same level of curiosity as, say, "confirmed bachelors" in those days. Nor it was safe for lesbians of that era to "come out." Even a hint of suspicion about Mary's love life could cost her job, her friends, her freedom (a great many non-gender conforming individuals in those days were institutionalized), and quite possibly her life. Violence against gay individuals was not only common but also frequently condoned by the police. In many cases the police were the ones committing the violence in the first place!

Legal or not, gay people did exist. And somehow (bizarrely!) continued to have sex and romance in their lives despite all the efforts to stamp them out. There was a thriving nightlife for lesbians in London's Chinatown and West End. Gerrard Street was an especially lively hub. Home to the 1917 Club frequented by Virginia Woolf, it was known as a day and night local for queer avant-gardists. There was also the Cave of Harmony set up by Elsa Lanchester, Smoky Joe's, Sandy's Bar, and Maxies Café. The two latter institutions which catered to more working-class clientele might well have been patronized by Mary while she studied nursing at Queen's.

Pamela Mitford of the famous Mitford sisters spent twenty years as the "companion" to Italian horsewoman Guiddata Tomasi. That they were lovers was an open secret in upper crust British society at the time, yet it was never publicly spoken of. Nor were any of the other "companionship" arrangements endemic in society at the time between two women or two men. As long as you were discreet, it seemed you could get away with anything. But heaven help you, if somehow you landed on the wrong person's radar. Alan Turing would be persecuted into suicide at the age of 41, despite the pivotal role he played in helping the Allies win World War II. Being a genius and a national hero didn't save him any more than being a genius and England's most celebrated playwright saved Oscar Wilde. This was the reality of the times for individuals like Mary Grey and her various lovers.

I chose to write a mystery in 1930s England for two reasons, the first being that all my life I've been an avid fan of classic murder mysteries, and inter-war England is rightly recognized as a Golden Era for detective fiction. It was the heyday of the Detection Club which sported such luminaries as John Dickson Carr, Dorothy Sayers, Baroness Orczy, G.K. Chesterton, Hugh Walpole, and, of course, the one and only Dame Agatha Christie herself. To write my own puzzle in such an era seemed only right as a way of paying homage to these great authors who'd helped pave the way. But I wanted to put my own spin on it. Something they would not have—and indeed could not have done—that I could.

The second reason I chose to write about the era I did was that it was one of the most fascinating time periods I could imagine. Many critics refer to books by Agatha and others of this time as "cozy" mysteries.

Besides the question of whether murder is in fact ever "cozy," these stories take place against a backdrop of growing darkness. The cloud of fascism was spreading all over Europe. A society for whom the scars of the First World War were still raw was about to get pummeled by another one. Some knew it was coming. Most were in denial.

And this is the reason for my other investigator: Mary's friend, mentor, and employer Franz Shaefar. It quickly became evident while writing *The Illhenny Murders* that Mary and Harriet would need an experienced hand in murder investigations to help them out. But it was equally evident this person could not be a practicing policeman. Ergo, a private detective, ideally one with a background in law enforcement. When Agatha Christie first introduced Hercule Poirot in 1920 (her most beloved creation to readers even if he was the personal bane of her existence), she was influenced by the rush of Belgian émigrés to England at the time. More than a decade later where I set my series, Great Britain was experiencing a high volume of German Jews fleeing the madness that had overtaken their homeland. They weren't warmly welcomed. Anti-Semitism was endemic in British society at the time, especially among the upper classes. Two of Pamela Mitford's sisters were openly sympathetic to the Nazi party. Diana Mitford married Sir Oswald Mosley, leader of the fascist movement in Britain. Unity Mitford was a close friend of Adolf Hitler, and when Britain declared war on Germany, she shot herself in the head. She survived but was incapacitated for life. Thomas Mitford, the sole son, had fascist sympathies as well and allegedly refused to fight in Europe. He was assigned to the campaign in Burma and died there. One can only imagine what Mitford family gatherings were like with three fascist siblings in the family; a lesbian; the great novelist Nancy Mitford, who openly satirized and mocked British fascists; and another sister, Jessica, who was a staunch Communist. (And they say American Thanksgiving dinners with Blue state and Red state relatives at the same table are awkward!) But the infamous division within the Mitford household spoke to a growing polarization and general sense of unsettlement within British society as a whole.

The "Hitler émigrés," as they would come to be called, weren't just looked on with distrust because they were Jewish, but for being German. The English have always been suspicious of visitors from the Continent. Anti-German sentiment especially raged high among the lower classes after the losses in the Great War. Shaefer is thus often suspected of being a German spy! We've all heard of the Japanese containment camps in the United States during World War II. What's less remembered is that England established internment camps as well for Austrians, Italians, and Germans and that many of those interned were Jewish. In fact, they made up a very high percentage of internees for the simple reason that

Jews were the former citizens of those countries most likely to have fled to England. The camps were located on the Isle of Man and other remote areas of England and Scotland. A total of 30,000 Jewish persons were held captive there until England decided the threat of an inland invasion was no longer imminent and "generously" released them. Another 8,000 Jews were deported to Australia.

The British immigration process at the time was designed to keep out far larger numbers of European Jews than it admitted. Shaefer, who begins *The Illhenny Murders* living in a state of dire poverty and isolation, would have been considered one of the more fortunate cases. For him solving the murder of Anthony West and others isn't just a matter of justice or even earning his fees. It's his only hope of having the means to rescue his family from Germany.

Thus was born the Mary Grey/Franz Shaefer partnership. Two very different people who might otherwise never have even met become fire-forged friends through their shared bond of being persecuted. Both their positions are precarious. Either one could easily be killed simply for being who they are. Mary at least can conceal her "Otherness" in English society in a way Shaefer cannot. But Shaefer at least enjoys the advantage of not technically being outlawed in Great Britain as he was in Germany. But official law dictated that no more than 5 percent of total students in any school could be Jewish. Jewish refugees who were licensed physicians were not allowed to practice medicine. British fascists routinely led anti–Semitic riots. Before the notorious Battle of Cable Street in London's East End in October 1936, there were the Battle of Tonypandy Field, Wales, in June and the Battle of Holbeck Moor, Leeds, in late September. Small wonder Franz Shaefer frequently wonders if he should go further abroad than England to find a new home.

Besides all the above I thought it might be refreshing for a change to have a male/female detective pairing where there was no possibility of romance or sexual tension. Mary and Shaefer's friendship runs deep but is by definition platonic. Rather like Will and Grace only with the female partner in this instance being the queer one. Of course, to the various people they meet, such emotional intimacy automatically raises suspicions of physical intimacy as well, especially given they're both unmarried. At various points in the books, Shaefer acts as Mary's "beard," a role he is happy to play!

A final note on why I chose the setting I did. I found the events of nearly ninety years ago to be distressingly relevant to current times. We like to tell ourselves we're far more enlightened today than we were back then. In some ways that's true; gay marriage is now legal in Great Britain. But bigotry and hatred are still all too powerful. Look at the national moral panic against transgender individuals. The legislation taken against transgender youths in Florida and Texas mimic the Third Reich's early attacks on the LGBTQ community. Among the Nazis' first actions was to raid the libraries of the Institute of Sexology and burn 20,000 books pulled from the shelves in the name of protecting Germany's youth from being indoctrinated into moral perversion. Across the globe authoritarian movements continue to gain power and too often it's met with complacency. Refugees fleeing political violence and certain death in their home countries are often greeted with hostility rather than empathy. When writing about Mary and Shaefer's world, I am consistently reminded of how much of it dovetails with our own.

Reading over what I've written, I realize I'm at risk of sounding overly didactic as well as grim. That was not my intent when I started writing this any more than it was my intent when I began drafting my first foray into detective fiction. Despite the gravity and vulnerability of my characters' situations, I try not to make my books unrelentingly bleak—quite the contrary; troubled times are when a sense of humor is most essential! Ultimately, like all authors in my chosen genre, my intent is to entertain and engage with my readers. If I happen to do so in a socially relevant way, that's just gravy. But murder mysteries, like all other books, are a reflection of their times, both those they are set in and those they are written in.

Postscript

I've Been Here Before

Phyllis M. Betz

My wife enjoys watching the Hallmark movie channels—the romance stories as well as the mysteries. As a storyline develops, I've seen her become fully engaged in the characters' lives; she applauds the happy ending of a romance, even if she's seen it several times. She recoils at a detective's danger regardless of knowing the outcome of the investigation. I, too, enjoy rereading detective novels that I have previously read. Agatha Christie's Miss Marple and Hercule Poirot mysteries, among other writers' works, remain favorites, and just as my wife still responds to familiar movies as though seeing them for the first time, I also put aside my previous knowledge of what happens and get caught up again in following Poirot's investigative skill in unraveling a complex case. We have not really forgotten what has happened in a revisited narrative; rather, we are suspending our past experiences with the novel or movie to immerse ourselves in the narrative as if for the first time. I can only describe it as a form of Coleridge's famous dictum about Shakespeare, that the audience (reader) must cultivate a willing suspension of disbelief. Knowing what we already know about a particular movie or text, my wife and I readily distance ourselves from that awareness and renew our acquaintance with the narratives.

Our experience with enjoying stories that we've previously read or watched is not unique to us. Many of my friends re-read authors and works they already know. Friends of mine reacquaint themselves with Christie or Sayers or Tey regularly. And this habit of re-reading is not limited to those of us who enjoy detective novels; another friend re-read Jane Austen's novels every summer. I have been asked why would I, or anyone else, for that matter, want to read the same stories over and over again. My response to this question rests on my understanding of certain critical ideas about how readers engage with texts. Although this sounds esoteric and too academic, I know that these concepts are not unfamiliar to most. I have shown students many times in introductory literature courses that they come to a text—even those who say they don't read anything beyond sports or fashion magazines—already aware of what is needed in a work to make it understandable and enjoyable. Such readers may not know the language, but they know the experience and can, when asked, articulate what supports their response to a work.

We keep returning to certain types of books, movies, and other media because we find in them some kind of satisfaction. That pleasure stems from seeing the puzzle of a mystery working to its appropriate resolution; the renewed appreciation of the author's ability in using the conventions; or the enjoyment in the choice of a particular writer or genre. This continued return to the books and writers we like is often criticized as lazy reading. Enjoying popular fiction becomes a sign of a reader who has a superficial understanding of how literature and serious texts are constructed. Popular literature is perceived as lacking innovation on the writer's end and mindless consumption on the readers' part because authors build these works on sets of conventional strategies. Negative critics regard this utilization of standard genre tropes as a crippling dependency that stifles innovation and dampens creativity. John Cawelti, one of the first academic critics to take popular literature seriously, has shown that to understand the purpose behind how these writers utilize the conventions of a particular genre, one must realize these works must be "treat[ed] for what they are: artistic constructions created for the purpose of enjoyment and pleasure. ... Because formula stories involve widely shared conventions, what one could call a form of collective artistic behavior, we must also deal with the phenomenon in relation to the cultural patterns it reveals and is shaped by, and with the impact formula stories have on culture" (2). The choices a writer makes are not guesses or ticks on a menu; rather they reflect a writer's knowledge of what a book, whatever the genre, needs to make the text work and what a reader looks for in such a text. What Cawelti points to is an understanding of the reciprocal exchange between book and reader, that the popular text embodies a society's conception of what is important as well as helps shape those ideas.

This means that readers actively participate in their engagement with a book: "Reading popular fictions is not a mindless and submissive process. One the contrary, it requires the constant exercise of one's interpretive powers" (Swirksi 70). What happens in this process centers on the reader's previous awareness of what a particular genre requires to distinguish it from others, how the writer utilizes those various conventions in the construction of the story, and whether or not the writer has balanced expectation with innovation in the incorporation of conventional requirements. Someone who enjoys fantasy novels, for instance, expects the novel to create a world where magic controls its workings, where dragons exist, and where heroes defy death to rescue others. While the representation of these tropes may vary, a reader who does not find the essential components of fantasy fiction will drop the book. The familiar conventions of popular fiction also serve, perhaps, a more important role. As my previous work on lesbian genre fiction shows, a lesbian author, by using the traditional conventions of the detective story or romance novel can position her protagonist in such a way that the reader, whatever the reader's sexual expression, can accept during the progress of the narrative. Kate Delafield, Katherine Forrest's San Francisco police detective, is a by the book officer who follows department procedures to apprehend the perpetrators in the cases she investigates. First and foremost, Kate is a police officer, and readers follow her investigations that adhere to the expected conventions found in every police procedural. Once the crime has been discovered, Kate and her subordinates take control of the scene, search for evidence, identify witnesses and suspects, carry out interrogations, deal with setbacks, and finally determine the perpetrator and bring the case to a positive conclusion. In other words, Kate Delafield behaves as every other police detective portrayed in movies, on television, or in novels does. By putting Kate into the police procedural format, Delafield must play fair with her readers' expectation that they will be engaged with a police officer's pursuit and eventual capture of a criminal. This must occur even though Kate Delafield is a lesbian.

However, what gives Forrest's novels their power is her descriptions of the constant friction between Kate's public and private lives; this is presented mainly through cases that focus on gay and lesbian victims and the overt homophobia of fellow officers and society as a whole. Not all representations of queer communities are negative, however; Forrest also gives Kate the ability to find a supportive community and shows the ups and downs of trying to maneuver a romantic relationship through an environment typically hostile to lesbians. How far can Forrest stretch the procedural format without turning the novel into a polemic? The typical reader does not want to be preached at or lose the thread of the investigation to what is perceived as distractions. Forrest achieves this balance as noted above by the plots of her novels but also by incorporating the social ideas about lesbian and gay people into the crime and investigation as well as by creating characters who take on the role of explanation or comment. These individuals, however, must be smoothly integrated into the narrative. For example, Maggie Schaeffer, the owner of the Nightwood Bar, fills the role of teacher to Kate; this is because Kate has deliberately closeted herself to advance in the police department. The murder has taken place outside of a lesbian bar that Maggie owns, and many of the regulars distrust all police officers, so Kate must find a way to gain their support. Maggie helps bridge the gap between Kate and the others. Over the Delafield series, Maggie reappears as Kate begins to accept and embrace her identity and helps Kate navigate the new world she now inhabits. As a result of Forrest's management of the requirements of the police procedural, she effectively presents readers compelling detective stories while still bringing to readers an awareness of the difficulties faced by lesbians and gay men when confronted by societal homophobia.

When authors utilize the mechanisms of popular literature to include serious questions or to represent social changes, they are participating in a process that Philip Fisher calls "making familiar" (19). Fisher's analysis focuses on three nineteenth-century authors—James Fenimore Cooper, Harriet Beecher Stowe and Theodore Dreiser—to dissect the processes at play that made their novels, once the most popular in the century, into works relegated to the backrooms of American literature. What I want to emphasize is Fisher's identification of the methods used by these writers, and, I would contend, modern popular fiction writers as well: "recognition, repetition, and working through" (7), which he asserts serve as "features of cultural incorporation. Only a few facts keep on being remembered as who we are and those facts are incorporated and then, after a time, felt to be obvious and even trite" (8). Certain subject matter Fisher notes, a slave's humanity, for instance, is more easily comprehendible when placed within the pages of the sentimental novel. I think Fisher's concepts become clearer with more recent examples. In 1977 the nighttime comedy *Soap* aired on ABC for four seasons; what is important for my discussion is that one of the major characters, played by Billy Crystal, was a gay man. In 2003, *All My Children*, one of the most popular daytime soap operas, showed two lesbians kissing. Interracial couples were often first seen on soap operas as well, and shows like *Julia, Good Times*, and *The Jeffersons* gave African American characters the primary place. Even the Hallmark Channel, with its rather conservative programming, has romances where the main couple are lesbians or gay men. Interracial couples are also appearing with more frequency. The Hallmark Mystery Channel has also branched out and presented Latino and African American detectives. What is most notable, for me, is that Fisher's main criterion—repetition—clearly references popular genres' reliance on standard tropes in the development of these narratives. The very factor that most negative critics dislike is the essential mechanism for bringing excluded people and situations into the foreground.

How does a reader know what the conventions of a police procedural, or any popular genre, are? George Dove notes "[t]he context of a detective story includes not only the text in the reader's hand but all previous reading, especially in the detection genre, together with the reader's preconceptions of structure, conventions, and rules" (40–41). In other words, a fan of police novels will develop an understanding of what is required for the novel to fit into that category due to a repeated reading of police procedurals. When those expectations are not met or handled poorly, the reader will typically know where the writer failed and may refuse to read another work by that author. Whatever the genre—mystery, romance, science fiction—this ability in the reader to recognize what components belong in a particular text is essential. Remember what Swirski said above—readers know what they want from a book and consciously select those works that satisfy their expectations. Critics of popular fiction also point to the perceived deleterious impact a steady consumption of such literature has. In the real world, they assert, love doesn't conqueror all and the case is not always solved. Repeated reading of popular fiction only serves to reinforce such unrealistic views of life. This attitude sees readers of popular fiction as robots that simply accept what is on the page; I would assert that most readers are, in fact, aware that what happens in the pages of a novel merely reflects the real world, even though a reader might hope that the criminal will be caught. I think when critics assume that readers of popular fiction have no ability to discern what separates a good text from a bad one they are engaging in a snobbery that privileges what they see as serious literature and that tends to look down on people who really like mysteries or westerns or science fiction. "We read on," Swirski notes, "to learn more about the story, to see our predictions thwarted or confirmed, or to devise answers to gaps, puzzles, or questions posed by the plot and the characters. In other words, we interpret popular stories cognitively, much as we do prestige fiction" (70–71).

Knowing what will happen in the story, however, does not infringe on the reading experience; in fact, such knowledge creates a sense of anticipation. The reader becomes an integral participant in the development of an investigation or a romantic relationship. We look for the familiar characteristics within the narrative to assure us that the story will achieve the required outcome. When an author tweaks the conventions, we are pulled up short because of the unexpected, but if the alteration still maintains the genre's traditional structure, we willingly accept the variation, which then becomes integrated into our history of reading. And the next time we take up another work in the genre, we will set it up against what we have come to already know.

WORKS CITED

Cawelti, John G. *Adventure, Mystery, and Romance: Formula Stories as Art and Popular Culture.* University of Chicago Press, 1976.

Dove, George. *The Reader and the Detective Story.* Bowling Green State University Popular Press, 1997.

Fisher, Philip. *Hard Facts: Setting and Form in the American Novel.* Oxford University Press, 1987.

Swirski, Peter. *From Lowbrow to Nobrow.* McGill-Queen's University Press, 2005.

About the Contributors

Carol E. **Ayer**, a Highly Sensitive Person (HSP), lives halfway between San Francisco and Sacramento with her cat, Rainn. She is the author of the HSP Mysteries published by Camel Press. Her website is http//www.carolayer.com.

Phyllis M. **Betz** taught English literature and composition for thirty-two years at La Salle University. Now retired, she has the time to read more mysteries and other books for pure enjoyment. She is also the editor of *Reading the Cozy Mystery* (McFarland, 2021).

Leslie **Budewitz** writes the Spice Shop and Food Lovers Mysteries. As Alice Beckman she writes moody suspense. A three-time Agatha Award winner, she is also a lawyer and past president of Sisters in Crime. She lives in northwest Montana.

Kait **Carson** (Kim Striker) is the author of two series set in the steamy, tropical heat of Florida. She lives with her husband, four rescue cats and a flock of conures in the Crown of Maine. Her website is www.kaitcarson.com.

Jennifer J. **Chow** is the Lefty Award–nominated author of the Sassy Cat Mysteries and L.A. Night Market Mysteries. *Mimi Lee Gets a Clue* was one of BuzzFeed's Top 5 Books by AAPI authors. She is the vice president of Sisters in Crime and active in Crime Writers of Color.

Maya **Corrigan** writes the Five-Ingredient Mysteries featuring a café manager and her live-wire grandfather in the Chesapeake Bay area. Each book has five suspects, five clues, and Granddad's five-ingredient recipes. *Library Journal* describes the ninth book, *A Parfait Crime*, "a riveting mystery with a sweet ending."

Tina **deBellegarde** writes the Batavia-on-Hudson Mysteries. The first book, *Winter Witness*, was nominated for several awards. Her short story "Tokyo Stranger" was nominated for a Derringer Award. Known as "the Louise Penny of the Catskills," she co-chairs the annual Murderous March Mystery conference. Learn more at tinadebellegarde.com.

Vicki **Delany** is one of Canada's most prolific crime writers and a national bestseller in the United States. Author of more than 50 novels (also under the name Eva Gates), she is the recipient of the 2019 Derrick Murdoch Award. She lives in Prince Edward County, Ontario.

Peggy **Ehrhart** is a former English professor with a doctorate in medieval literature. Her Maxx Maxwell blues-singer mysteries were published by Five Star. She now writes the Knit & Nibble mysteries for Kensington. Visit her at www.PeggyEhrhart.com.

Mary Anna **Evans** is an associate professor at the University of Oklahoma. She is the co-editor of the Edgar-nominated *Bloomsbury Handbook to Agatha Christie* and the author of fifteen crime novels that have received recognition including the Oklahoma Book Award and the Will Rogers Medallion Award.

Amanda **Flower** is a *USA Today* bestselling and two-time Agatha Award–winning author of more than forty-five mystery novels. She has also been nominated for a Mary Higgins Clark Award. A former librarian, she and her husband live in Ohio with their adorable cats.

Winnie **Frolik** is the neurodivergent author of the Mary Grey series with Nine Star Press. She resides in Pittsburgh, Pennsylvania, with a very demanding cat named Smoky. When she dies, bury her heart at the Main Branch of the Carnegie library.

Marni **Graff** is the award-winning author of the Nora Tierney English Mysteries and the Trudy Genova Manhattan Mysteries. Her short story "Quiche Alain" is in the Anthony Award–winning anthology *Murder Most Edible*. She is the managing editor of Bridle Path Press and a crime book reviewer.

Sherry **Harris** is the Agatha Award–nominated author of the Sarah Winston Garage Sale Mystery Series and the Chloe Jackson Sea Glass Saloon Mysteries. She is a past president of Sisters in Crime and a member of Mystery Writers of America.

J.A. **Hennrikus** has worked in arts administration for more than thirty years and is the executive director of Sisters in Crime. Her tenth novel, *The Plot Thickens*, written as Julia Henry, was published last fall. She also writes as Julianne Holmes. Her website is https://jhauthors.com/.

M.E. **Hilliard** is the author of the Greer Hogan Mysteries, which feature a crime fiction–loving librarian sleuth in the fictional village of Raven Hill, New York. A former business executive, she is a professional librarian living in southwest Florida.

Andrea J. **Johnson** is the author of the Victoria Justice Mysteries, a courtroom whodunit series. She teaches creative writing at the University of Maryland Eastern Shore and authored three guidebooks: *How to Craft a Killer Cozy Mystery*, *Mastering the Art of Suspense*, and *How to Craft Killer Dialogue*.

Sybil **Johnson** is the author of the Aurora Anderson mystery series, craft-based cozies set in the world of decorative painting. Her short fiction has appeared in *Mysterical-e* and *Spinetingler Magazine*, among others. Originally from the Pacific Northwest, she wields pen and paintbrush from her home in Southern California.

Kathleen Marple **Kalb** (Nikki Knight) describes herself as an author/anchor/mom … not in that order. An award-winning weekend anchor at New York's 1010WINS

Radio, she writes mystery short stories and novels including the Old Stuff and Ella Shane series, both from Level Best Books.

J.C. **Kenney** is the Amazon, Barnes & Noble, and Kobo bestselling author of the Allie Cobb Mysteries and the Darcy Gaughan Mysteries. His debut, *A Literal Mess*, was a finalist for a Muse Medallion from the Cat Writers' Association in mystery fiction. His website is www.jckenney.com.

Justin M. **Kiska**, when not devising clever ways to kill people (for *his* mysteries), is a theater producer and director. He is the author of Parker City Mysteries from Level Best Books and the creator of Marquee Mysteries, a growing interactive series. His website is www.JustinKiska.com.

Edith **Maxwell**, an Agatha Award–winning author, writes the Quaker Midwife Mysteries and short crime fiction. As Maddie Day, she pens three other series. A member of Sisters in Crime and Mystery Writers of America, she lives north of Boston. Find Edith/Maddie at https://edithmaxwell.com.

Rabbi Ilene **Schneider** is a retired Jewish educator and hospice chaplain in Marlton, New Jersey, where she spends her time birding, gardening, streaming, traveling, over-sharing on Facebook, and writing the award-winning Rabbi Aviva Cohen Mysteries, short stories, and non-fiction.

Diane **Vallere** is the national bestselling author who writes funny and fashionable character-based mysteries. After two decades in luxury retailing, she traded fashion accessories for accessories to murder. She started her own detective agency at age ten and has maintained a passion for shoes, clues, and clothes ever since.

Index

Milton Keynes UK
Ingram Content Group UK Ltd.
UKHW031448310724
446381UK00014B/94

Applying Performance